ALL DOGS DIE
Alle Hunde sterben

CW00541950

ALL DOGS DIE
Alle Hunde sterben

a novel by
Cemile Sahin

translated by
Ayça Türkoğlu

—— MTO PRESS
WIVENHOE 2024

We see a tower block in Western Turkey. The block has seventeen floors. Each floor has six flats. There is a lift. A cellar, but no attic. We're in the stairwell. It's dark. Uniformed men enter from the left-hand side of the frame. They charge up the stairs.

15:44

EPISODE ONE: NECLA

> Necla lives on the ground floor. Necla has pitch-black hair. Necla has a dog. Necla doesn't want to stay here.

I've never been one to hold back. I report on everyday life. I've talked about the things I know. Perhaps not exactly the things I've seen, but still, I've always told the truth. I often stand in my kitchen, behind the table, behind the curtains. The things I see usually only happen outside my door, on the street. It's almost like a film. But I can't fast forward or rewind, or press pause. I live on the ground floor and I live alone. My name is Necla and over my socks, which are very warm, I wear a second pair of socks, woollen and extra thick. I wear them so I can creep about my flat like a spy. I live alone and I hold my breath as I walk around. Who might hear me? The neighbours could hear me. Which of them has heard me already? All of them. The same thing happens whenever they hear me: they think about me, and that reminds them of everything I've done, then they hate me. They hate me because I cause them harm. What do I do? Something I've been doing for years now. I betray my own people.

What does that mean, betrayal? Betrayal is the opposite of death. It's insurance for life. I want to keep living, really I do. I don't want to die.

I've lived in this tower block for eleven years. I had a dog when I first came here. My dog's name was Bero. Bero, time to eat, I'd say. Then I'd set a bowl of meat on the stone floor, and Bero would eat until there was nothing left. When Bero was done eating, he would sit there staring at the bowl. Bero, you've already eaten, I'd say. Bero would give a yelp and I would laugh, pick up the bowl and put it in the sink. That's all there is, I'd say. Just like that, the bowl's empty again. I think about Bero and that bowl a lot, you know. An empty bowl in the sink is a fitting description for my life. I came here on foot.

It doesn't matter how it happened. What difference does that make now? I had my dog on a lead. We live on the ground floor now. I don't know where my kids are. But I do know where my dog was. My dog was lying on a blanket that I knitted by the stove before I left my house behind. Bero was a Kangal. His muzzle and his ears were dark brown. The rest of his body was beige. When Bero stood next to me he came all the way to my hips. He wore a collar I'd knitted for him, a red one.

One day, a watchman came to my home. I thought it was the neighbour when I heard the knock on the door. I had a glass of tea in my left hand and I turned the handle with my right hand and said, smiling, *Fatma, you're early.* But when I opened the door, it wasn't Fatma; it was a man. He was wearing a uniform. His hat didn't match. Neither did his belt. At first he smiled at me, then he knocked the tea glass out of my hand.

Where is he? he yelled.
Who? I asked.

He stripped off my dress, my shoes and my socks, until I was in my bare feet. I can still remember it clearly. He pulled a rod out of his belt; I thought it was a fork at first. He hit me in the face. And then he beat the soles of my feet. He kept going until my feet burned. That was the first time I cried out. My dog Bero came running in from the other room. Then the watchman hit my dog too. I lay on the floor wondering if the man was a policeman or a soldier. My dog yelped because the metal rod had struck him too. Bero tried to snap at the watchman, but the watchman held him back by his collar as the tears ran down my cheeks. The watchman overpowered him even though my dog weighed more than fifty kilos. I weighed seventy kilos – more than my dog, less than the watchman – but we were already trapped.

The watchman grabbed me by the hair and pulled me out of the flat. He dragged me down the steps, through the gate and into the yard. It was a small yard with three cars parked in it. The rubbish was piled up in a heap; there is no waste collection service. Bero's kennel was next to the rubbish heap. My husband had built it years ago but Bero had never used it. We'd always let him stay inside the flat. I liked the kennel though. It was red, like Bero's collar.

The watchman dragged me along. My stomach hurt, my legs too, the concrete was uneven and the asphalt scraped against my skin with each tug towards the kennel. When we made it to the kennel, the watchman turned my head back towards the tower block, then to face the kennel. And once he'd done that, he slammed my head into the ground. It made me woozy.

Don't move, he said.

Out of the corner of my eye, I watched him walk over to one of the cars and open the door, then come back holding a plastic bag. In the plastic bag was a collar on a chain. He put the collar around my neck. He wound the end of the chain twice around a piece of wood and hammered it into the ground near the kennel. Then he squeezed me into the kennel. I'm a grown woman, and the kennel wasn't small but it wasn't big either. I had to tuck my legs in to fit inside.

The watchman said, What do we do with dogs like you?
I looked at Bero and started to cry.
No, no, he said. Not him, he said, pointing at Bero, I mean you.

He was still holding Bero by the collar. It had been getting thinner and thinner – I thought it would tear in two like a rope under the weight. But I also thought that if it did, that would be a good thing. Then at least Bero could run away and be saved. Every person who can be saved is one more person. Yes, my Bero was just a dog, but still.

Then the watchman shot at me. It wasn't until the ninth shot that I realised he was only shooting to frighten me. He had no intention of hitting me. I screamed *BERO*, because I my children's names didn't come to mind. The watchman still had his hand around my dog's neck. And I knew he was doing it deliberately. There was rubbish in the kennel, too. It smelled like it did outside. But I didn't notice the smell until the bullets shot past me. Only in the hail of bullets did I think of the stench.

I had two children, two. I forget that sometimes. Please don't laugh at me. I forget because they're not here, and I forget how long it's been. A life can be very long. I was in this kennel. First, winter came. Then spring. There's only one story to tell from my life in the doghouse: whenever the watchman came, I had to crawl out of my kennel and wait on my knees in front of him until he hissed, Get up. At first I fought back, but at some point I stopped. Not because I didn't have the will, but because of a simple fact: if I did what he said, I'd get less of a beating. It helped me to survive. No one wants to die like that.

I didn't know where the others were. I was all alone, wearing a collar, in a kennel, chained to the ground. Why? Then he made me stand up and salute him, right hand on my temple, and yelled, KEEP YOUR HAND STILL, until he started laughing, STILL, STILL! and forced me to my knees again. This went on for hours. To keep from losing my mind, I kept count in my head. One. Two. Three. Even when he hit me. I tried to cling to the numbers. Four. Five. Six. This was how the time went by. Seven. Eight. Nine. My arms and legs began to cramp up. Ten. Eleven. Twelve. He didn't need to explain himself to anyone. I thought about how he wanted to kill me.

He said, Eat, you whore.

He threw a plastic bag at me and I looked at the plastic bag as if it meant something to me. Then the watchman took a rat out of the plastic bag, a dead rat, and there was a piece of meat, grilled meat. I couldn't tell what kind of meat it was. It was pale, perhaps it was chicken. He threw the pale meat to my dog. The watchman and I, we watched Bero eating. And as my dog ate, he held him by the neck. Bero's knitted collar still hadn't torn. I was very glad about that. It was the only peaceful thing in that moment. Then he picked up the rat by the tail and tossed it at my feet: Eat, he said. I didn't take my eyes off him, but then he took a step towards me. Only then did I see the rat on the ground. That was in the winter.

The rat lay in the snow, I knelt in front of it. The watchman let go of Bero's neck and grabbed mine instead. I wanted to cry out but I couldn't because that would have meant opening my mouth. He pushed my head back and used his other hand to pry open my mouth. I didn't scream until the rat came closer. Then the rat was in my mouth and I wanted to vomit. It was a rat, it was dead; I was chained up and my mouth wouldn't close. I was full of disgust, for myself and for Bero, but my disgust didn't change a thing about the situation. I couldn't breathe. I gasped for air, thought about something else and tried not to swallow and struggled to breathe again and I thought I'd suffocate. The same thing happened to my husband. He was in prison in the eighties. He only talked to me about it once. Now it's too late to think about his story. The watchman put one hand on my head and the other on my chin. Then he forced his two hands together until I bit into the rat and had to swallow. I can't remember much else about it now. I fell to the ground, perhaps I fainted, but he wanted me to keep saluting, my knees were blue with cold, then I fell asleep.

Then one thing happened after another. I heard machine guns and I looked at the watchman, who didn't know what was going on either. He came over to me, kicked me in the stomach, in the face, tied my dog's collar to my collar, and ran off. The noise grew louder and I started to grub away at the ground to free my chain from the piece of wood. Why hadn't I thought of that before? Why hadn't I started digging when I was freezing in the kennel at night? I dug and I cried. I thought about the rat and I cried. I saw a woman digging with black-bruised fingernails like a dog, chained to another dog, showing no sign of stopping. I saw a woman and I thought about her hair, which had fallen out. I kept digging until I started to smell smoke. I dug faster and I was still chained up. We both saw what happened, I said to Bero.

I reached for a big plastic sack and threw it over myself, like a jacket. Bero, I whispered. Come here, Bero. Then we fled. We were both emaciated. I placed my hand on my dog's neck, like the watchman had, and stroked his knitted collar off his canine body. On the way here, I tore his collar into lots of little pieces. I dropped the pieces on the way to help my children find us if they make it and come looking for us.

My children weren't at school the day the watchman came. I had known for a while that someone would come for us. One evening, I packed their things. My elder son was eleven at the time. I can't say his name because I forgot it out there on the street. And this part of the story is worse than the rat I was forced to eat. I packed my son's bag: a few pairs of underpants, a couple of pairs of socks, two pairs of trousers. I rolled his clothes up like a baguette so that they wouldn't take up too much space in the backpack. Then I rolled up two jumpers I'd knitted and put them on the top of the other clothes with a picture of our family and a comb. The zip moved slowly along the opening. I did the same for my second son, my eight-year-old.

It was still dark outside but I woke my children and dragged them out of bed. I helped them put on their socks, their trousers, vests, shirts and jumpers. Then their jackets. I packed them as much bread and cheese as they could carry. Then I gave them all the money I had left, walked them to the door and hugged them for a long, long time. I smiled so that they wouldn't cry. I tried to act as if everything was okay, but of course, it wasn't okay. Now you're wondering how I could do such a thing – yes, I know that's what you're wondering. But there's no simple answer. Write that down. I don't know if there's even an explanation.

Our house was there, in the place we called home, and I stood by the door in the middle of the night with my two children, and the crickets were screeching, and I sent them off to another city, to my brother. My children started to run because I said, You have to go. There's only one way to survive violence, to be stronger than it: by protecting your children. Yes, that's the only way.

I knew the watchman was coming; I just pretended to be surprised when he arrived. But I was fully aware that they were looking for my husband. My husband's name is Ferhat. Ferhat is a kind man. While they searched for my husband, they had me shackled me to the ground. We are dragged out of our homes, then we disappear. So, here we are, the watchman said to me. I tried to ignore what he said, tried to memorise his face instead. To not forget a single line, a single hair.

I thought: *I'll be back someday*. I was certain: *I'll get him back for this someday.* And I won't even do it at night; I'll do it in broad daylight for everyone to see.

But I never went back. I've been living here on the ground floor for eleven years, waiting for my children to arrive. I live on the ground floor so that my children won't have to walk up the stairs. I live on the ground floor; that way, I can just open the door and run if my kids turn up and I see them coming. I didn't even run when I escaped from the kennel. I would run for my kids though. And for my husband. I live on the ground floor so that I can sit by the window in my chair every day to look out onto the street. If my kids were dead, I would know it. And I think it's a good sign that I've spent eleven years waiting for my children; it means I know that they're safe. Every day that passes reassures me that they're alive. If they were dead, my brother would have called me, but I haven't heard anything from him for eleven years. And not hearing anything is a good sign. Because it means they've found somewhere to hide. I imagine simple things: that they're safe and don't have to sleep on the floor, that they have proper beds. I hope my sons live long and healthy lives.

Around here, I speak to no one. I don't like going out. I don't have anyone to tell about what happened. Ferhat said that in prison they want to break you. They want you to kill yourself so they don't have to do it. I'd love to talk to my husband, Ferhat, but I don't want to tell him what happened. I'd like to watch a film with him and tell him what I think of it.

I couldn't stay there anymore, of course I couldn't. The whole place had been torched. I was wearing a dirty plastic sack and all I could save was my Bero, my starving dog. The watchman had hacked off one of his legs, but thankfully the wound had healed. Bero had got used to having three legs, just like I had got used to the kennel. People can get used to anything. Animals adapt to hardship, too.

I didn't meet anyone on my way here. I was full of lice. *Serves you right,* I thought. My husband's cousin, Ayten, was living here already and took me in. I knocked at her window one night. I tried to say her name but it had been so long since I'd spoken that only a whimper came out of my throat. I could hardly understand myself. *Ayten, Ayten,* I scratched at the windowpane. At first she thought I was a burglar; she was frightened when she saw me outside the window and I still couldn't bring myself to say her name. She only realised it was me when she saw Bero. HIS LEG, she screamed. I was holding Bero back by the scruff, the same way the watchman had done.

Ayten put me in the bathtub. I think I must have sat in that tub for two days, the filth clung to me. My skin was black and blue, the veins in my legs had burst. The lice jumped off my head and into the water, then they jumped onto my back and bit me. Ayten had to shave off my long black hair, I'd always loved my hair so much. It was only then that I started bawling and finally called out my children's names.

Ayten made up a bed for me. It was the first time I'd seen a normal bed in eight months. Bero lay down at the foot of the bed. It was the worst night of my life. I was no longer cursed with being outdoors; for the moment I was safe at a relative's house, under a warm blanket in a warm space.

One day a man came to see Ayten. By that time I was no longer living with her and had moved onto the ground floor. You know, it's obviously very practical for us all to be in one place. There are at least six flats on each floor. And if we're all in the same place, they can control what we do. And what we don't do. Policemen come and say, You can't all leave the country. But I don't want to leave the country anyway; I have to stay here to wait for my children.

When my kids come back, we'll wait for my husband. And when my husband gets here, we'll leave this tower block. I know that lots of people have left. I don't know how they did it. Some struck out on their own, some went in groups. Sometimes they would have to separate on the way. Bero and I, we can't do that. Bero and I, we wait in a room in the flat.

A man, his name was Murat, came one night. He was a tall, gaunt man with a big black moustache. His face was bruised. He had a plastic zip-up laundry bag on his shoulder, it was pristine. Ayten was afraid someone would see us. She pulled Murat into her flat and turned off the lights. Then we had to sit on the floor. Have you seen them? I asked, as quietly as I could, but Ayten punched me on the shoulder, grabbed me by the neck and said, Don't shout, Necla.

When she grabbed me by the neck, it made me want to take another swing at the watchman. Murat said my husband Ferhat was up a mountain, surrounded. The mountain is beautiful and has four peaks. Each of the peaks is over 2000 metres high. Murat said my husband wasn't with my children; he was with my brother. My husband was up a mountain but he was surrounded by soldiers. A bullet had hit him in the arm. Murat explained that my husband Ferhat had slumped down not long after that. The other men thought he'd fainted, but then they noticed that his right leg had given way because a bullet had struck his leg too. He and three other men dragged themselves into a cave and hid. This was a few months back. Is he dead? I asked. No, said Murat, he left. My husband Ferhat had set off to reach my brother so that he could be with our children. That evening, I lay in bed and thought about what the air must be like when you're 2000 metres high.

I wondered whether Ferhat's breathing was better or worse up there, what with the bullet wounds. I got up and went to ask Murat. I crept into his room in the dark, but it was empty. Then I went into Ayten's room and shook her awake. She was frightened at first, but then she calmed down.

Where is he?
Gone.

I let go of Ayten's neck. I sat on the edge of her bed and sighed. Where did he go? Ayten sat up. She just shrugged, then she said, The two of us are here. And when she said this to me, I realised that Murat, the man with the bloodshot face and the plastic zip-up laundry bag on his shoulder, had come to Ayten's flat perhaps out of pity or kindness but hadn't had the heart to tell me the truth. When Ayten started to cry, I finally understood. And Ayten started to cry because in that moment, like me, she had understood too. My husband Ferhat hadn't left to be with our children. My husband Ferhat was hit by two bullets: one in the arm and one in the leg. My husband Ferhat died on a mountaintop, 2000 metres high. It's impossible to imagine such a thing. It's impossible to invent such a thing.

I sank to the floor and squeezed myself under Ayten's bed until I fit beneath it. I was trapped, like I had been in the kennel. That was when, finally, I whispered, My husband. Ayten tried to drag me out, but I dug my fingers into the bedframe. Ayten pulls at my dress and I scream: *Ferhat.* She keeps pulling harder and harder; my dress tears in two because Ayten is pulling on it and I'm pulling on the bed and neither of us is letting go. I pay close attention when my dress tears. It's the sound I was so scared of. It's what I thought was going to happen to Bero's collar in the watchman's hands. I hear the sound and then I scream my children's names. I want to bury my husband Ferhat, but I don't know which mountaintop he is on.

At some point, Bero comes into Ayten's room, lies on the ground next to Ayten and looks at me. I say: I'm going to find him. This is what I say to Ayten. But the thing is, and this I'm now saying to you, I have no idea where to start looking. Ayten lit a candle. I started knitting. First I want to knit a blanket for my husband to be buried in. When I'm done with that, I'll knit a collar for Bero. Finally, I'll knit a blanket for myself. If I die soon, I'd like to be buried next to my husband. Shrouded in a blanket, like him. Then I told Ayten about the rat. She threw up and I carried on knitting. Then I noticed how grey her hair had turned; I kept knitting and I had no idea how long my own hair had grown over time. But I didn't put my knitting needles down to run my hand over my hair. I couldn't tell how long I'd been there. So I kept knitting because that's my answer to this life.

The next day, I decided to go to see my brother. I wanted to fetch my children. And go somewhere else. I said, Ayten, we have to leave this place. I went down to my flat. I stood in the stairwell and said, We've all got to leave this place, we have to go home. But I didn't really know which home I meant anymore. The home without my husband but with my kids? Or the time before that? If I had to choose, I'd choose my children. None of this is their fault.

What's the time? What day is it? My neighbours think I'm spying on them because I the only one I speak to is Ayten. A soldier came by once and started a rumour that I was working for the government. He was probably about as old as my elder son is now. I stood stock-still next to him. I kept still when he beat me, too. Perhaps he was my son? No, I would have recognised him. I take back the story I started with. Forget what I said before. I wasn't lying, I just can't tell someone everything all at once. Yes, I creep through my flat in two pairs of socks. But not so that I can spy on my neighbours; it's how I survive the time that has to pass before I can hold my children in my arms again. I creep through the flat wearing two pairs of socks and there's something I understand well: behind a door is a room, and beyond the room is a wall. And on the wall hangs a flag, and when we see their flag, we know which country we're in. We're in this country. And if a soldier sees us here, he'll grab us and make us stand in front of their flag.

I took my duffel bag out from under the bed. Then I packed my things. I filled it with the same things I'd packed for my kids: trousers, socks and underpants, two knitted jumpers. Then I looked at my belongings for a long, long while before unpacking the bag again and tucking it under the bed. I realised then that there's nothing I need; I just have to run away.

Then the doorbell rang all of a sudden and I jumped. Who was at the door? Ayten never rings the doorbell. Ayten always uses my spare key to get into the flat. That's how I knew something was wrong. I automatically looked over at the window but my bedroom looks back out over the yard. There was no one there, ringing the bell. Then I walked to the front door ever so slowly. I didn't know whether to open it or not. At first I considered hiding under the bed. But they'd find me there; it's a stupid hiding place. I held my breath as I looked through the spyhole and into the corridor. I saw Ayten, which surprised me. It wasn't until I looked closely that I could see the outline of another person on her left. Then the doorbell rang again. Oh no, I said, oh no, not making a sound. I felt Bero nudging my leg with his muzzle. Then I opened the door.

It reeks of smoke in here, says the man next to Ayten. Is he talking about my flat? Or my husband? Did he burn my husband? He must have shot my husband, I think. Ayten's eyes are glassy. She has a gun in her hand. Her hair has wrapped itself around her necklace.

I want to say: Ayten, what are you doing? But Ayten won't look at me. The man says, Shoot, Ayten.

But Ayten looks past my shoulder at the ground and I can't work out what's going on. I think about the watchman's hand on my dog's neck. My Bero is standing next to me, the man steps towards me, then he gets behind Ayten and grabs her by the shoulders, squeezes.

Shoot, Ayten, he says again.

I think of my husband Ferhat's blanket, I feel sad that I probably won't get to finish it. Shoot, Ayten, the man begins to yell. Nothing happens at first, then he grabs her hair and pulls her head back with her hair in his fist. Ayten's hair is her noose. I want to run over to her, but when I see her necklace break in the scuffle, my eyes follow the necklace, which falls to the ground. The man shouts. I put my hands over my ears. His mouth is moving but I can hardly hear a thing, thank God. Thank God, yes, no one's burning. Ayten turns the gun on me but I'm not angry with her. Ayten has tears running down her cheeks. Then she pulls the trigger and I've closed my eyes. I let myself fall to the ground and I think I'm saying something or screaming this time, but the words always come too late and only then do I realise that it's not me screaming.

Ayten has shot my dog. He was standing behind me, by my hip. My dog howls, my dog Bero without his collar, my dog with three legs. He howls and I've never heard anything like it before. What have you done, Ayten? and it hits me extra hard. The man grabs Ayten by the back of her head and slams her face against the wall. My little Bero is still howling and Ayten is standing between me and the man, leaning against the wall, covered in blood. Eventually my dog gives one last wheeze. There's nothing more bitter in the world than listening to someone die, even if it's just a dog. I take one last look at my Bero and then he is still. Ayten slumps to the ground and hides her face in her dress.

The man grabs me by the arm. Now he's trying to drag me out of the flat. I fight back and let myself fall to the floor. He says, Where is your husband, Necla? Where is he? *On a mountaintop, that's where,* I think.

Ayten, I whisper, please, Ayten. You've got to bury Bero, please. Take the blanket I wanted to give to Ferhat. The man is bigger than me, he grabs me by the arms. Who betrayed us? He pulls my arms behind my back. Where are my children? Ayten, I yell, I don't know if she can hear me. What's wrong with her? I ask the man and turn to look at him, and he headbutts me.

Ayten, wait for them, and by them I mean my children. Ayten, please bury Bero, Ayten, let him have some dignity at the end. Use the blanket, Ayten. Ayten, I forgive you. I'm not angry with her. I told her that. He drags me out of the flat. I have nothing else to say.

17:12

EPISODE TWO: MURAT

> Murat lives on the ninth floor. Murat has a plastic
> zip-up laundry bag. Murat doesn't consider himself
> a hero. Murat doesn't want to stay here.

Things work a bit differently around here, you say. But that doesn't mean all we do is suffer. No. That's not how it is. We talk about the violence we've experienced. That's the only way to fight back. So that the story dictated by the military doesn't become the only story that everyone in this country believes. It's like this: soldiers hunt us in the streets, in our flats. That much is certain. You tell yourself: Everyone understands. It's instant. That's how these stories begin. But my father, my sister and my brother didn't disappear with soldiers, no. They disappeared with other men. Men in this country often have jobs like that. Spies, we call them. Terrorists, they call us. I call it violence in its worst form.

Spies show up in cars. Soldiers come in tanks or buses. Spies wear suits. Soldiers wear uniforms. Spies are part of a special unit. An underground operation. If any of them denies it, it means he's got his reasons and is one of them. And if he's one of them, he won't give himself away. You don't know when they'll come. But you know one thing for certain, and it's that they'll come eventually.

It's a simple equation: soldiers wearing uniforms in tanks and buses can be spotted from far away. We're prepared for them. Everyone knows: if you wear a uniform, you're announcing yourself as a soldier. Or a man from a different unit. But a man in a suit, getting out of a car – he could be anyone. And if anyone could be anyone, then how are we supposed to know who the spy is? But the thing is, we do know. A spy is always well camouflaged. His clothing doesn't stand out like a soldier's uniform, not at all – a man in a suit blends in. And so, the line between spies and residents blurs. And when that happens, you can't tell spies and residents apart. It makes life complicated.

A man stepping out of a car in a suit brings a spell of uncertainty with him. Uncertainty, because with each man in a suit, a picture of anxiety sneaks in. There's only one part of the picture we can think about: the spy is among us. Because any suit could belong to a spy, since all suits are worn by spies. And every spy is a man in a suit who may have stepped out of a car. The spy motif becomes its own tale. Because that is the story's starting point: the man in the suit getting out of the car. The tale takes on a sequence and the tale has a story of its own.

This is how it begins:
1) I see a man in a suit.
It goes on:
2) A man in a suit gets out of a car.
It continues:
3) A man in a suit watches me leave my house.
The story always begins outside your own front door.
You tell yourself:
4) Today could be the day.
You speculate:
5) Today there will be a man in a suit standing outside my front door.

Or even:

6) They will come today; the men in suits always look different.

Waiting.

Spying.

Boom.

Gone.

But the question is: when will the spy reveal himself? You tell yourself: The spy will reveal himself when he has done his job. Simple as that. Unfortunately, this is not always true. Sometimes, he just won't.

WHAT HAPPENS THEN?

That's when it gets really hard. Because you'll never find out which of the men in suits was the spy. And so you ask yourself then: Who betrayed me?

It wasn't long after sundown, but it was already dark. That's something you need to know: it always starts when it's dark.

The soldiers say, Terrorists come at night. But we come first. I'm telling you: a house stood there, with another house next to it and then another. My father, my sister and my brother were all in my house. They disappeared at the same time. By that logic, it means they all disappeared together. In a nutshell, it means I wasn't standing far away from them. There was a house there too, and in front of the house was a man, in a suit, who had stepped out of a car. He stood beside my father and my siblings. They were almost in a straight line. I only noticed his gun right at the end; it appeared from under his jacket, below his chest. I'll summarise: there was a spy in a suit with a gun by a car next to a house. Only then did I realise it was serious. My father turned his head, yes, trying to find me; he looked to the right and stopped when he spotted me in my hiding place. It's me, I wanted to say. My father was shorter than me, with a big moustache, just like me; we looked straight into each other's eyes for five seconds, he and I. Then he bowed his head without saying a word.

The man in the suit who had got out of the car forced them into the car he'd arrived in. The car had four doors and the windows were tinted. The car was white, but since you couldn't see into the windows, the white car became a dark car in my mind. These days when I see a white car it automatically makes me think of a dark car. It's only when I think of the car that the suit appears, and with the suit comes the man in the suit, getting out of the car.

In my hiding place, I put my fingers in my ears. You tell yourself: That's what they all do. By which I mean spies. The car drove away. I climbed out of my hiding place. I ran out onto the street, where the car no longer was, just other cars and the house. The woman from over the way, she came running too; she grabbed my arm and took me into her flat. I was twenty-five at the time. I could hear the sound of the car engine in my head. I threw myself onto the ground. But the ground wasn't what my father had looked at. The street was the ground and my father and my siblings drove away in a car, over that same ground.

Then I ran away. Where did I run? To my mother's grave. My name is Murat and I ran straight to my mother's grave. Tanks were driving through the streets. I saw soldiers. I saw them jumping down from buses, from tanks, and charging through the streets one after another. By then, my father and my siblings were gone. The tanks were big and dark. The soldiers moved around the place without talking to each other. I can't remember what colour the buses were. Which soldiers came from the military base nearby? Why were they here? Which soldiers had arrived on the buses? Why did they come that day? You tell yourself: That doesn't matter. What mattered was that soldiers from two different places were mixing.

A soldier came. Followed by another. And another. A soldier stood in front of a car in the street, and on the street in front of the soldier was a house. As soon as you noticed one, there would be another standing behind him. It all happened faster than you could describe. Each of their assault rifles is part of the sequence of this story.

Gun.
Detonator.
Ammunition.
Gloves.

I saw it myself. Everyone sees it. Everyone knows it, too. But still everyone wants to believe the truth. And the truth is, a special unit was charging through our streets. A special unit equals violence and humiliation. Put more simply, it means one person doing harm to another person. Deliberate harm. There is no accidental harm. Violence with assault rifles means sleeplessness. During the day. And at night. Anyone with an assault rifle can shoot. And if you don't have an assault rifle, you just don't have one. You tell yourself, It's that simple.

I saw the soldiers and I thought of my mother. Straight away I feared for her. The tanks drove towards us. Street signs toppled over. Civilians were throwing stones at the tanks. Then at the soldiers. I threw a couple too.

One of them said: You're the children of whores!
I thought: *The law arrives by gun.*

They have to go back to their barracks with good news. And good news is only ever news that involves numbers. Numbers are used to count dead terrorists. Nothing else. But in the army's eyes, half the country are terrorists. You wonder if they all really believe the same thing.

I didn't care much about them hunting us. My biggest worry was the graves. Tanks and buses drive wherever they please; they've no need for roads, and the government builds those anyway, and the government does as it pleases in this region. And the tanks create new routes of their own and those belong to the government too. So you stop being able to tell if you're standing on a road or not. Everything looks the same. By which I mean: flattened. Don't get me wrong. Soldiers have an aim and they have a mission. The aim and the mission are the same. It all involves us. But then you look at what's happened. Undergrowth, flattened. Road signs, valleys: flattened. Streets, graves: flattened. The government built the roads but the tanks don't drive along the roads; they deliberately take other routes, over graves.

I mean, how can one person face down soldiers in buses and tanks? What can one person – me in this case, the person telling you this – do to counter this violence? I'm not a victim and I don't want to be thought of as one; it's the people listening to me, the ones who can't believe what I'm saying, who make me a victim. Not me. Write that down. Victims are killed. I'm still alive. Victims can't fight back. I fight back by talking about it. I'm telling you all this, but what can be done to fight it? Does talking about it make it stop? Or does it stop once I've talked about it? I'd have to say no. I don't even need to wait for your reply, somehow I just accept reality.

If you start running, they run after you. They've got their gear on. It's heavy. It normally weighs between twenty-five and forty kilos, but they're used to it. It makes no difference to them. Violence is what keeps them going. Their reality consists of attacks, terrorists, traitors to the fatherland. Our reality consists of the same things. We all live in this country, after all. They're doing their military service. It's possible to get out of it if you have enough money. That means you won't have to waste your time in the army. But the sons of poor families, for instance, they can't get out of it. Others just go AWOL. Some of them get caught because the authorities go looking for them. So in the end they all do their military service. And they have to do it to protect their fatherland. And they don't just protect it on either side of the border. No. They say: The enemy is living among us. By this they mean that traitors to the fatherland are damaging the nation from the inside out. They say: We're monitoring you very closely. Which means: violence is what's holding the fatherland together too. You tell yourself: That's obvious.

So, you run away from them. And if you manage to lose them for a moment, it's not true freedom, it's not happiness, it's not an escape. No, it's only temporary. Because this time, the story goes like this: The soldiers come again. They get out of their buses and tanks. Until they've got everyone.

Do you want me to die?
Yes, they shout.

They beat me unconscious. The next day, they forced us out of our homes. It was only then that I remembered my mother. And so, I went out the door. Turned left onto the path outside our house. Kept going. Left again. Up a hill. Straight ahead for a time. A car. Then right. It was getting light. Kept going. Then right again. I knelt on the ground when I got there. Then I was on all fours. I called for my mother but she didn't answer. I called again, very quietly; I was scared my mother couldn't hear me. You tell yourself: No one can hear you. But I had to call out quietly so that the soldiers wouldn't find me. Tanks had driven over the graves. Of course they had. It made it hard for me to find my mother's grave. You tell yourself: Everything looks the same as it did. That's violence, too. And all sorts of symptoms overwhelm you. Everyone gets them. You lose your sense of taste. Your hair falls out. Swollen hands. Water collecting in your legs. It's not nice.

Then I did something. It wasn't nice either, please don't judge me, I know what it amounts to, I've already got enough to deal with, but it was something despicable, everyone would judge me, yes, I know they would. I dug her up. Out of the earth, I mean. I've never told anyone this. It's a mystery as to why I'm telling you now. Maybe because it's impossible to bottle everything up. I opened my mother's coffin. I dug my mother up. My mother died before my father and my siblings were taken away. I shut my eyes as I opened the coffin. There was no smell anymore. I was sure it would smell. Dear God, how could I think such a thing? Then I opened my eyes and it wasn't my mother I saw but her bones. I could hardly bear it. I flew into a panic and slapped my hand over my mouth as though the soldiers were at my back, as though they'd uncovered the shame I carried. It was a strange displacement activity. I lay flat on my belly next to the open grave, like a sleeping dog, and cried with my hand still over my mouth. You tell yourself: This is what you've become.

In these stories, the sequence goes like this: First they charge through the streets. Then they will haul us out of our homes. Then they will set my home alight. Whether I'm in it or not.

They say, When a house burns, terrorists die.
You tell yourself: And time keeps marching on.

Houses burn from the outside first. Then from the inside. It depends where they start the fire. And then, eventually, the people inside burn too. In one burning house, for instance, my mother's sister died. My mother almost fainted. Her sister's hair caught fire. It didn't smell at first. She always said, There was nothing there. Then her sister's hair began to smell. My mother would never be free of that smell. My mother is buried near her house. You tell yourself: It won't let me be. So you talk about it. Please don't get me wrong: I didn't open my mother's coffin for nothing.

Once I was over the initial shock, I carefully closed the coffin lid. Then I went back home. I vomited, first in the garden and then in the kitchen. At some point, I sat down on the kitchen chair, at that small blue table, and vomited again. Then I started cleaning the flat. When I was done, I opened the cupboard under the sink and took out a big plastic zip-up laundry bag from the back corner. Do you know the ones I mean? I keep saying plastic zip-up laundry bag, but I mean those big, tough bags you can fit a lot inside. Then I ran back. At first, I was cursing myself. You're saying: What has got into you? But no one came to help me. And then I took the bones out of the coffin, one after the other, and packed them slowly, carefully, into the plastic zip-up laundry bag. Nothing happened at first. But then I thought about what I'd done.

I've just escaped. I climbed up a tree as the tanks drove past. Then I climbed down. Then I made a run for it with my mother's bones. I was being so cautious as I ran that my progress was only slow. What worried me most was the thought that the tanks were going to turn around and catch up with us. Drive right over me out in the street with my mother over my shoulder.

I can't tell you how long I was on the move. One evening, probably weeks later, I reached a rocky clearing in the woods. I was starving hungry. Horribly thirsty. The plastic zip-up laundry bag was unscathed, but I was completely worn out. I carefully placed the bag on the ground and inspected it closely. Then I took a rag out of my rucksack. It had been so long since I'd seen another person, I didn't know how I'd ever manage to live in a city again. Then I hung the rag around my neck, it became a noose, and I thought, *Now I'm going to take my life.* The rag smelt mouldy and I thought, *That's another problem, but this is where I belong.* Am I really that savage? I'd say yes, given that I've packed my mother's remains into a plastic zip-up laundry bag and it's sitting right there in front of me. I thought, *I'm punishing myself for the injustice that's been done to me.* I thought, *I'm punishing myself for my thirst and my hunger.* With this thing around my neck, I jumped down from the branch of a tree I'd climbed. I was gasping for breath. It wasn't a nice feeling. I was still the same person up there in the air. But if the soldiers had found me, they would have said, *He's a terrorist, let him die.* Yes, let him die. Because this time the terrorist didn't ambush them; this time he'd hidden his mother's bones in a plastic zip-up laundry bag.

You have so little left and you tell yourself: If you die now, your mother's bones will be stuck inside a plastic zip-up laundry bag. You'll be hanging from a tree until your strange noose eventually breaks under your own weight and you drop to the ground. Even then, you might land on the plastic zip-up laundry bag and crush your mother's bones.

In a situation like this, you think: *What's become of you?* You talk to yourself a little and say: Nothing has become of you. You can't picture a future for yourself. You tell yourself: Your mother's in a plastic zip-up laundry bag. You're dying tied to a tree. Soldiers use the same tactics: they tie their terrorists to trees, too. They don't use nooses, they usually shoot terrorists in the head.

I became someone else. I stopped talking about this betrayal; with my mother in the plastic zip-up laundry bag I practically switched sides and became the betrayer myself. Just before the end, you tell yourself: Where you fall depends on where the noose breaks. Then you tell yourself: It wasn't soldiers or spies that did this to you this time. And you're angry with yourself. You think you've bowed to their story.

I whirled my arms around because the noose was squeezing the air out of me. I thought smoke was coming out of my head, but the smoke was coming from the houses. I was close to fainting. Please, please, I wheezed as my throat closed tighter. You tell yourself: You're wearing dirty clothes, even your noose stinks. Please, please, you say again. Then I heard the noose tearing slowly above me. Please, please. Then I was hanging almost by a thread but the thread was still strong enough. I was still dangling there. I tried to spit, tried to make space for myself. I started to swing from left to right, couldn't move forwards, kept trying. You say to yourself: This rag's already half-throttled you. I must have marks around my neck already. That was my one hope. You say to yourself: I don't want to die here. And if you don't die here, it'll be a small mercy. The mercy isn't God's, I'm godless. And you say to yourself: But in this country piety helps. Twenty soldiers take on one civilian. This is when you understand the extent of what's possible in this country. And this is when the soldiers understand it for the first time, too. You tell yourself: Go ahead and shoot! Who was I speaking to? There was nobody there. Something inside me had blown. ARE THERE OTHER CASUALTIES, I shouted. It's pointless. I'm not a hero. No. Who'd want to die a hero's death these days? Only idiots would want such a thing. Did you know that when men are shot they die as soldiers? Only traitors are hanged. It's important to know the difference. In this country, you're either a hero or a traitor. There's nothing in between.

At some point I fell to the ground. Mercy. I lay there, I'm not sure for how long, until I stopped wheezing. You tell yourself: So, I've survived this, too. By which you mean: That's one way to keep your morale up. Then I went over to the plastic zip-up laundry bag and carefully looped the strap back over my shoulder and walked on. Write this down: What I'm trying to say is, soldiers are biased. They don't hang you from a tree, they shoot you dead.

Eventually, I arrived in a city again. I fished some old clothes out of a bin. This is what it's come to, you tell yourself. And you say: What a disgrace. New trousers (dirty), new jumper (dirty). I sat down in a café, I had no money. I sat there for over thirty minutes. Eventually, a waiter came and set a bowl of lentil soup down in front of me. *He feels sorry for you because you look so wretched*, you think. The TV was on and there were only men in the café. They watched me come in and when they'd had their fill of looking at me they turned away. They were probably thinking,

He's not from around here, we can tell.
He's an outsider, we can tell.

The men saw the fire on the TV. But they didn't understand that I was sitting near them with my mother on my lap and we were also watching what they saw. We peered up at the image on the TV until the next one appeared. We watched images from the place I had left behind. The newsreader said, Right here. And you say to yourself: Where's 'here'? We all saw the smoke streaming out of the windows. The men said: God protect our soldiers. And I squeezed the handle of the plastic zip-up laundry bag. One house had yet to catch light, it caught fire next to a house that was nearly caving in. I'm sorry but this time we got away just in time, I wanted to say, but instead I said:

Write this down: Smoke brings dirt with it.

The men at the other tables, they shook their heads. Clearly they hadn't understood. One of them laughed and said: He looks mad. He must be mad. I wasn't mad. But what's mad is how fast houses burn when the army sets the fire right. I stood up. Then I ran away. And this is where I ended up.

I live on the ninth floor. I share the flat with a man. I have a bathroom without a bath, but there is a small shower area. The bathroom has no windows. In front of the cupboard is a chair, and on the chair, which is brown, there are trousers, shirts, jumpers draped over the armrests and piled on the seat, so you don't immediately notice the cupboard door, behind which my mother lies in a plastic zip-up laundry bag. I live with Haydar. Haydar is probably as old as me. We're probably the same height, too. At least that's how it looks when we stand side by side. Haydar has a moustache and he still has a lot of hair on his head. When I wake up in the morning, Haydar is already up and dressed. Then he sits on a chair. The chair has its back to the door. Because Haydar sits in the chair and watches the street. If you were looking at him from behind, you'd just think:

1. THIS IS A PEACEFUL SCENE

You'd probably think:

2. WE'RE LOOKING AT A MAN.
3. THE MAN IS SITTING ON A CHAIR
    WITH HIS BACK TO US.
4. THE MAN IS PROBABLY LOOKING
    OUT OF THE WINDOW.

Then you'd say:

5. THE MAN IS LOOKING OUT OF THE WINDOW.
6. WE DON'T KNOW HOW OLD HE IS.
7. BUT WE KNOW HE IS SITTING ON
    THE CHAIR QUITE PEACEFULLY.
8. THE MAN ISN'T WEARING A
    SUIT, SO HE CAN'T BE A SPY.
9. WE CAN'T SEE HIS LEFT ARM.
10. THE MAN IS BREATHING CALMLY.

We can't see this, but we can hear it.

But if we were to take a few steps towards him in order to observe him from the front, then this peaceful scene, which we've described solely from our own standpoint, would conjure a different picture. And this picture would tell us something different. Then we'd understand that our description doesn't fit what is actually happening. We'd be presented with two different images which, like a spy and a soldier, have nothing to do with each other on the surface. If you were to walk up to him slowly, he wouldn't turn around – that much is certain. But what might happen is that we'd see:

11. THIS IS NOT A PEACEFUL SCENE. IT'S REALLY
    NOT.

You'd probably think:

12. WE'RE LOOKING AT A MAN, JUST AS BEFORE.
13. THE MAN IS SITTING IN FRONT
    OF US ON A CHAIR.

Perhaps now you would start to describe the chair, to get a better picture of the situation. But then again, perhaps you wouldn't. To do so would be unnecessary and would add nothing worth knowing to the plot. And this description wouldn't tell us any more than we already know.

But the truth is:

14. WE SEE A MAN GAZING OUT OF THE WINDOW.

After looking at the man, we would also glance out of the window. But like him, we wouldn't see what he wanted to see. We'd see nothing. We would then turn back towards him, and only then would we notice the gun in his left hand. A black gun, lying in his lap. He won't talk and he won't explain. The man sits calmly on the chair, looking out of the window.

I ask him, What is it you're doing?
Waiting, he replies.
I ask, What is it we're waiting for?
To that he says nothing.

I watch Haydar every day. Sometimes he comes into my room and then I get up and get him something to eat. He sits on my bed and waits until I come back with a plate in my hand. I sit down next to him, give him the food and wait until he's finished. Haydar's hair is dark brown. When his plate is empty, he says, Thanks, and I know he's had enough.

Haydar and I are waiting for different things. I'm waiting for the time to pass until I stop worrying that someone will find the plastic zip-up laundry bag; that's why I try to only concern myself with Haydar and to block out the things I know about myself. I watch Haydar every day, so sometimes I actually forget about the plastic zip-up laundry bag in the cupboard behind the clothes on the chair. You tell yourself: Today is a new day. I'm grateful for that. I no longer see the chair that conceals my hiding place; instead, I return every day to the room where Haydar sits and, I now know, looks out of the window with his back to the door. But I've forgotten to mention that his other arm, not the gun side but the other one, also has a part to play. If you approached Haydar from the other side, the picture you'd see would tell a different story. An observer – me in this case – would only notice at second glance, and I only noticed very late, that the hand with the gun in it was not the important hand. Because everyone in the world knows what a gun is and, above all, what a gun means; in storylines where nothing else happens, they're often seen as the greatest threat. But only for that moment. Soldiers use the same tactics. When they're armed and you're not, it's not the soldiers who pose a threat. What I mean is: of course they're a threat, but the bigger threat comes from the guns that they carry and point at you. You tell yourself: I can see that. But then you forget what it's really all about because now the gun is all that matters. In this country it's about defending the country, which means guns are all about killing, but for Haydar, it's about something different.

If we hadn't attached so much importance to the gun in the first place, we would have seen the picture that Haydar was holding tightly in his other hand. His right hand is a fist and inside the fist I can see half a head, not quite tucked into his grip. At first, I didn't dare to ask what kind of picture he had squashed into his palm. I thought it might be someone in his family. A friend or an acquaintance. I didn't dare ask because Haydar would sit there for hours on end clutching the crumpled picture, his knuckles white. I observed this for some weeks and I also admired him for his courage because I thought – even though we're here and everything's gone to shit – Haydar sits here day after day with his back to the door and he has a mission, even though I don't know what he's waiting for. But I understood that he was at least waiting for something. I think Haydar knows about my plastic zip-up laundry bag but says nothing, out of politeness, because he knows it would weigh me down, and as I talk about this and think about him asking me about it, I feel hot and cold all over. You tell yourself: No one's found me out. I can't explain what possessed me, not even to myself.

At some point I started taking a chair out of my room. Not the chair with all the clothes on it, another chair. I took the chair into the room where Haydar was sitting, then I placed the chair next to Haydar. Haydar didn't look at me as I did this, which I took as proof that he had nothing against me being there. We sat side by side for weeks, saying nothing. From morning to night, until we went to bed. We looked down onto the streets; when uniformed men ran through the streets, Haydar's breathing would turn heavy. At first I spent a long time sitting next to the hand with the gun in it as I thought it might help me work out what was in his other hand. But I couldn't see anything from that side. At some point I switched to the other side. This didn't bother Haydar either. I knew because once again he didn't say anything about it. Haydar looked out the window and I looked at his hand with those white knuckles. Sometimes I wanted to hold his hand because I thought it must be hurting him.

Then I asked him: Are you waiting for the person in the photo?

Haydar stared out of the window and nodded. For the first time since I'd known him, he opened his right hand. Then I saw his fingers; between his fingers was a photo and in the photo was a man. I couldn't really make out who he was. The picture was so faded, I squinted and wondered how Haydar would manage to spot this person on the street. There was barely anything to see. The photo was so crushed that the colours were smudged and the paper was worn in places. Haydar must have had the photo for years. I have to correct what I just said. When I look again, I can make out the outline of a person. There's a man in the photo. Yes, that much is definite. There's a man but nothing else. The man's face in the picture is fuzzy, which makes it hard to guess his age. But I think he must be as old as me and Haydar. There's a man, trousers, jumper, jacket. You say to yourself: This man isn't a spy. His hair hangs over his ears but doesn't go down to his chin. In the photo, he's smiling at the camera.

Who is that? I ask Haydar.

A policeman, he replies, but I can't understand how he knows, because the man isn't wearing a police uniform in the photo.

On the back of the photo are the words:

You should go to Germany
And not come back
There's nothing here

For a second I thought, Maybe Haydar's been watching too many gangster films; I know I shouldn't joke, but I'm not actually joking. We always watch gangster films together in the evenings and I laugh at the pathetic dialogue, but I know that there's something weighing on Haydar – no matter how he speaks or stresses his words – and I would never laugh about it, because madness is what's driven us both. You tell yourself: It's true, of course. I have a plastic zip-up laundry bag in the cupboard with the chair in front of it, how can I be free of it. I can only guess at what might be weighing on Haydar's mind. The men's uniforms get to him, they get to all of us, it's something none of us can escape. But you know, I can only bear things if I can laugh about them.

What if he doesn't come? I ask softly.
Then I'll go and look for him, he says.

How can Haydar rely on the photo? All it shows is a man. How will Haydar be able to recognise him on the street? And what if the man never comes? What then? Haydar can only wait for what he thinks he sees in the photo. I can only describe what I see. Our days go by like this. Every day, we wait. This tower block is like a camp. We sit stacked on top of one another almost like animals and, though we don't want to admit it, we know we won't stay here forever. I never leave this room. Neither does Haydar. In every room of this flat there is a wall. In every room is a door. Not every room has a bed, but almost every room has a window.

One evening, I place another chair covered in clothes in front of the cupboard next to the other chair with clothes on it. Haydar and I are both anxious. For days, the raids have been relentless. We're only spared them until uniformed men come thundering through our door and we suffer the same.

When the knock at the door came, I knew they had come to take one of us away. That's what they'd done the day before on a floor below ours. Then I went into the hallway and watched them storm through the door. A spy walks in and points at you. You say to yourself: They really are everywhere.

Why do you people cause nothing but trouble, says the tallest of them. You tell yourself: One of us has to go first. Get as many of us as possible to safety later.

I look through the hallway, through the door into the other room, to Haydar. We won't see each other alive again. Haydar is sitting on his chair with his back to us, just like he does every day. It's a peaceful image. Write that down.

If Haydar were to ask me now, Did we really see that happen? I'd say, Haydar, everyone saw it. Then Haydar would be sure to ask himself, Was it in the East? Then I'd be sure to say Haydar, It happened here. Right here.

02:39

EPISODE THREE: NURTEN

> Nurten lives on the seventh floor. Nurten is not
> angry, Nurten is cool-headed. Nurten thinks about
> the future. Nurten doesn't want to stay here.

I come from a small village. It's really not big at all. Everyone knows everyone there. It's where I was born. My mother, too. Not my sister. We're simple people. We had a patch of land. It wasn't big, but it was enough for us. That's where our house was. Next to our house there was a stable, and in the stable were our animals. Sheep, chickens, horses, and donkeys. The rest of our family lived on the other side of the border. The border between here and there is 367 kilometres long.

The soldiers say, Terrorists use the border region as shelter.

My name is Nurten and I'm fifty-five years old. I have four children. One is dead and three are in prison. We haven't done anything wrong. You have to believe me even if you hear something different. I said to my husband, his name is Hasso, I said:

I have four children but they're all gone.
Hasso said, I know.

My three sons are scattered across the country. They're in different prisons. I can't visit them one after another. I can't see them all at once either. I have to decide who to visit and when. Agit is in the North. Erdem is in the West. Mahir is in the South. I haven't seen Agit or Mahir for years now though. Our visit requests were rejected. I tried to find out why but I got no answer. Instead, I was arrested and spent a few months in prison myself. I didn't care. And I have to say, but please don't take this the wrong way: I have no interest in talking. What I mean is, I don't want to start with me. I'd rather talk about my sons. My dead son, Hüseyin, is not in the North or the West or the South. I mean, he's not near any of the prisons. Where are we? In our minds, we're with our sons in prison: North, West, South. That's how it is. We live here now, not anywhere else. But we're not from here. I'd never been here before. Our relatives aren't from here either. Our relatives are buried somewhere different. Hasso and I, we want to be buried next to our relatives. The last time we tried to go home was with my son, Hüseyin. He was in his coffin and the coffin lay on a pick-up truck and the pick-up drove over the badly paved road and as we drove him home the road magnified the days that passed without my son in them – I mean, because he'd died – and my son, in his coffin, he was knocking against the coffin in the pick-up and I thought it would hurt him, so I said:

Hasso, please don't drive so fast.

We wanted to bury Hüseyin next to his relatives but we weren't allowed to travel all the way to our relatives with our child's coffin. We were stopped. A unit stopped us. There was nothing unusual about this. When you look out of the window all you see are badly paved roads; everything is a little run-down. You slip back in time, thirty or forty years. Life isn't all that pleasant because there's nothing left in the region now. Which means you can really see the difference. But you don't actually pay attention to what's around you; instead, you notice the things that stick out to you. And when you look at what's around you, the soldiers are usually what catch your eye. They're everywhere. You notice them soon enough. They're in front of you, behind you. To your left and to your right. Then you stare at them. What I mean is, you're so immersed in it by now. But to be honest, by the time we were sitting there in the pick-up, things were already very different. In Hasso's head and in mine, I mean. We were struggling with different things. We thought of the children and we thought about how we could change our lives. When you think about things like that, you're the last person to see what's in front of you.

They say: Terrorists creep out of every hole.

What they mean is that the people they see as terrorists are hiding in the mountains. We sat in the car and all around us it was very rocky. There were lots of mountains. I like mountains. Even as I child I liked them; I haven't changed in that respect. Some days I feel glad when I notice qualities in myself that I had as a child. Then I think, there are still things I can hold onto. And it's lovely to recognise things from the past. But only when they're good things, of course. We were stopped and searched. Hasso had to roll down the window and a soldier came up and stuck his head through the window; his face was almost touching Hasso's and Hasso gasped and the soldier didn't like that one bit, so he took his gun and held it up to the window and pointed it at us. At me, actually, because he couldn't point it at Hasso as he was almost touching Hasso's hairline. We were buckled into our seats and we didn't even have our jackets on. No, Hasso and I, we were both in t-shirts. Hasso's was grey and mine was white. The soldier said: Are you hiding explosives under your clothes? We didn't answer because we knew it was a rhetorical question. And the more you hear rhetorical questions, the quicker you spot them. And the more often you spot rhetorical questions, the quicker you can reply with your own rhetorical questions. Are you soldiers? I said. We had to get out of the car. Me first – because I was lippy, the soldier said – then Hasso. They made us stand in front of the car and started searching us. And they're very rough when they search you. Not all of them, but most. The soldier who searched us was not a sensitive man though. Sometimes I don't understand what it's all in aid of. He could just use his brain. What I mean by that is: he could, for instance, talk to us in a normal tone of voice. But they always yell as soon as they open their mouths. Why do they yell? I hate people who yell all the time. It's rare for me to yell. They unrolled their flag over the bonnet of our car. Then one of them forced me and Hasso to kiss the flag. You can't do this, I said. Then we kissed the flag because we were all alone on the road and I was scared that Hasso would suffer if we spent too long there, standing on the road between the two soldiers. When I kissed the flag, I shut my eyes and prayed to forget the image of it, prayed not remember it. And I thought, if I shut my eyes, there wouldn't be an image branded on my memory because I didn't see it in the first place. What I mean by that is: you only see what you want to see. And that's the same everywhere.

Hasso and I, we were wearing t-shirts; it was June and we were standing in the road like the chickens in our coop at home. We had to keep standing by the flag while they walked around our pick-up. One of the soldiers climbed up onto the back of the pick-up and pulled aside the blanket that had been covering the coffin. Everyone badmouths you and everyone who does is right to, I said. One of the soldiers standing next to me smacked me in the face, but it didn't make things any better and they pointed their guns at the coffin. Even in a situation like this, I didn't shout. No, because I've got a cool head. And anyone who shouted in this situation would only be shouting out of desperation. But I'm not desperate. No, I'm cool-headed. Write that down: Nurten is cool-headed and she doesn't shout. That's something everyone ought to know. I know it already because I am who I am; I'm not anyone else. I don't have to pretend for anyone.

But these things still happen. Then they opened our son's coffin because they suspected us of smuggling a terrorist into the mountains, hidden in a coffin. Soldiers don't have a shred of decency, I'm telling you. Really, everyone needs to know. Write that down.

Tell everyone you meet. Everyone needs to know. We've known it for a long time.

They said, This is as far as you're going.
I said, Who did this to you?
Then they said, If we catch you again, you won't be so lucky.

In their world, that meant we couldn't be allowed to go any further. And because they threatened to shoot us right away, we really understood what they meant. So, what can I say? Yes, we turned around. Hasso and I got back into the pick-up, turned it around and drove back. At first they followed us for a while and I said, They've really got nothing better to do. When they finally turned their car around, I said to Hasso, Let's stop here. Hasso said, But we're on a road. There's nothing round these parts. I didn't really like it, but if we'd driven back, or if we'd tried to get past them, we'd have had even bigger problems. I said to Hasso, We'll make the best of it. Yes, and I'm telling you, we did make the best of it, because that's how you think about the future. Hasso and I got out. Hasso grabbed the spade from the back of the pick-up. I pointed to the nicest spot I could see near the road and said to Hasso, Here. Then Hasso started to dig a hole. We only had one spade and we had to take turns. One of us would start to dig and the other would watch for a while. Then we'd switch places. You should know, we're no spring chickens these days, Hasso and I. It took us a good while.

Hüseyin now lies buried in the middle of a field on the side of the road. It's not far from home, Hasso, I said. I don't think Hasso and I will be able to go to visit him again. Our home is now a restricted zone. And restricted zones are guarded and monitored by the army. First they cleared our village and then they pushed us out. The army thought we might hatch a plot against the state from a tunnel we'd supposedly built several kilometres under the ground. But what would an underground tunnel do? You can't hatch a plot with a tunnel. Why are you doing this? I asked. But the soldiers didn't answer. Instead, they kept digging, laying mines and then covering them back over with earth. Terrorists always go back to their hideouts. And when they get home, the mines will blow them sky-high, one of them said.

Now we've ended up here, in this tower block. This is a part of my life. What I mean by that is: the different sections of my life have become a part of me. But it's not that tragic when you think of the future. This place isn't on fire. That's good. There are lots of us here. That's both good and bad. I miss my home, I can't lie. But I've stopped counting the years since we've been here. I mean, I know what year it is and what month it is, of course. I don't mean it in an ordinary sense. But time passes slowly, then it passes quickly, and suddenly the time has been and gone. And I don't know what I've done with it. Is it ten years that have passed? Or twenty? The tower block is like a chicken coop. We're stacked one on top of the other. It feels like a punishment. I just don't understand what we're being punished for. Some days, Hasso is sick with worry. Because of the children, because of the chicken coop, or because of this punishment. They blend together. The same happens to me. But I don't want it to happen. Hasso doesn't speak as much as he used to. We've changed too, my Hasso and I. But I always tell myself that's normal. People change over time.

When Hasso sits on the sofa and stares at the living room ceiling, I can see that he's in prison inside his mind. I was watching Hasso once and I don't know how it happened, but our donkey suddenly popped into my head. Not that my Hasso reminded me of our donkey, no, not at all. But I suddenly found myself wondering: what happened to the donkey in our stable? Then I asked Hasso.

He'll have gone home. They all go home, Hasso said.
But where's that? I said.

Hasso has nightmares because of his time in prison. He was in prison a few years ago. What you need to know is, people who torture people are no longer people. Seriously. My husband is a former prisoner but he will forever be that man in prison. The years go by, but that doesn't change a thing; I guess that's why I sometimes forget how many years have passed. I don't say this to Hasso though. My husband is scared of boots and my husband is scared of doors. I've taken all the doors in our home off their hinges. Hasso wanted to get rid of the front door too, but I managed to convince him to keep it. It's a red door, a nice door; red is a good colour. I've never lived in a house without doors before. Neither has Hasso. In the past, I would never leave the door open when I walked into a room. It didn't matter what time it was. What I mean is: I used to shut every door that I opened behind me. It's curious; sometimes I don't feel safe without doors anymore. I feel I'm being watched because I can't close the door behind me. But doors remind Hasso of prison, especially the sound of doors opening or closing. In prison, the door outside the cells would creak before someone came into the cell. And whenever the door creaked, someone would come up to the cell and then boots would come into the cell. And what the boots brought into the cell with them was torture.

Hasso said, If we don't have doors, I can see what's going on in the other rooms.

I thought he'd lost it because there was no one in the other rooms anyway. Hasso and I were the only ones there. And Hasso and I, we'd spend most of the day together in the same rooms. Our three sons were gone. Where were we? Nowhere close to the prisons. I try not to cry in front of Hasso, but when he thinks about Hüseyin or our other three sons, then he thinks about the torture again.

It's not clear why Hasso was kidnapped and tortured. Hasso was selling flour and soap in the border region. He'd been doing it for ten years.

But one evening, soldiers came and arrested all the sellers in the border region and stuck them in a cell without another word. I'm there for Hasso and he's there for me, but when we think of our sons we can't seem to find a solution. Hasso imagines our sons suffering what he went through, only worse. Sometimes I think what Hasso says must be true because Hasso knows what he's talking about.

And Hasso says, I hope they've not got cells with squeaking doors.
The future will be better, I tell him.

Then I usually go into the kitchen and bake bread. I can't think of anything better to do. I can't bear to see Hasso in this state. How can I undo the torture? I often ask myself the same thing. But I know I can't undo it. I'm stuck in this tower block. I look across the kitchen into the hallway without its door and I watch Hasso two rooms away, with only the hallway between us; I watch him sitting on the floor and staring out of the window. Hasso is slowly getting old. I stare at the kitchen around me. I think: My husband is a lump of damage. My four sons are too. When I get angry I say, This tower block stinks worse than a chicken coop. Why are you all squatting on top of each other like this? Go outside.

You know, when you're in prison, at some point you start smelling like the prison itself. Hasso for instance, he doesn't smell like Hasso anymore. Hasso went to prison, but the man who came out a few years later, he wasn't my Hasso anymore. You can't escape it. He was gaunt and all covered in lumps and blotches. I thought he'd collapse as he walked along. He coughed and wheezed when he spoke. His little toe was missing. I thought, Anything's better than this. Things will be better in the future.

Wherever the bullet strikes, that's where it hurts, the soldiers said. *That's true*, I thought. Hasso, I said. And Hasso and I, we set off.

Prisons are very dirty. Usually they don't have toilets. There's a plastic bucket in the corner that everyone has to share. It's humiliating. But imagine you're the sixth prisoner in a cell no bigger than six metres squared and you're forced to crap in front of everyone else. Prisoners are also forced to eat faeces. And they have to lick and kiss the boots of the men who kick them with the same boots they licked and kissed. Once you've gone in, you never come back out. I mean, you do come out if you're lucky, but the question is, how? How do you come out again? Since Hasso has been like this, I've said, Prison completely changes people. Six square metres for more than six prisoners. They have to take turns lying down. The only drinking water they have drips from the ceiling and the walls. They're forced to lick water droplets from the walls. Prisoners are human beings, after all, and they're thirsty. But everything's muddled in there. There's never enough of anything. Sometimes in the cells they have nothing to drink for days on end. Only when it rains. But it doesn't rain very often there. The prisons stay dry. Sometimes I thought Hasso would die of thirst in there. But Hasso didn't die of thirst. Even when it rained it still wasn't enough and the prisoners weren't people anymore. I want to keep a cool head, but when you know about these things you can't tell what the future might bring. Somehow, the future stops making sense. What I mean is: the future is small, and prison is big.

Hasso said: More people actually died of thirst than from torture. It was almost like peace.

I don't know if that's true. I don't think it's true. I thought he was making it up from the beginning. I thought, perhaps he cut it down so much in his head that the number of people who were tortured was eventually less than the number who died of thirst. Tortured people become numbers. Who counts the dead? My Hasso counted them. I think he says that for the sake of his conscience but I'm sure it's not true. My Hasso says it because it was his last hope against torture in the cell. My Hasso is a good man. My Hasso has scars on his back. You mustn't lose hope.

He said, When the door creaked, everyone flinched.

A man in a uniform would step into the cell. The prisoners had to undress and lie close next to each other on their bellies on the floor. In a tiny cell like that. The men were almost stacked on top of each other, like the branches of a tree outside our stable. The man who opened the cell door walked over the men's backs. There were steel hooks attached to the soles of his boots. Hasso thought the man had made them himself. With these hooks, he walked from one back to the next until the men lying on the floor bled and passed out. If any of them screamed from the pain, they would be punished with the steel hooks again. The man with the hooks on his army boots, he shouted, We are all proud citizens of this nation, as he tortured them. Who counts the dead? Not these men, that's for sure. But my Hasso counted the dead. He saw it all. And one day, he wrote the number on a piece of fabric and tied the fabric in knots until the number could no longer be read. Then it made a ring and Hasso hung the ring on the tree outside the tower block and said, At least this way they're outside. Oh God. The only thing that helps is thinking about the future. Honestly. But Hasso carries it all inside him and I can't get it all out of him. Who saw it? They all saw it. And this is how the torture continues. When I don't know what more I can do, I start baking bread. When I busy myself with something, I feel calmer, by which I mean not angry. There are twenty kilos of bread dough in the fridge, I tell everyone that. I say, It's for the future.

Not all prisons are the same. The prisons in Europe are humane, they're almost hotels. You have a cell, even if it's small, and you don't have to be cold. You get a window, even if it only looks out onto a wall. You get something to eat, even if it's not tasty. No one has to starve. There's water to drink; you get a bed, a blanket, a bedsheet, a pillow. Over here, they throw you in a dungeon. Hasso lost his hair in the dungeon. First his skin went yellow. Then green. Blue and purple, too. He showed me photos of it but I shut my eyes. It's damp in the prisons, it stinks of decay and people start to smell too. They become animals. Not horses but dirty donkeys. Donkeys are worthless; when they're old and smelly you shoot them. I wish my sons were in prison in Europe. I'd know they were safe there. Not all prisons are the same. Write that down. We look towards the future and the future is a prison in Europe. Do you see what I mean?

The woman on the ground floor, her name is Necla. Sometimes I take her bread that I've baked but she doesn't accept it. She works for the government, they give her money. She uses the money to feed her children, who are far away. Her husband's gone too. I don't know where he is; maybe he's in prison or dead. Hopefully, he's in prison in Europe. I don't wish ill on anyone. Except people who do wrong by others. I don't talk to Necla. Necla doesn't talk to anyone. Necla isn't from round here either. I don't know if she really works for the government. But there are people who will do anything for money. Even sell their mothers. That's when you think, there's so little people won't stoop to. But it's true. I mean, there are also lots of us who let ourselves be bought and don't care one bit. But if that's how they see their future, then they have every right to. We would never do that, Hasso and I. Write that down, please. I want everyone to know.

One day a soldier came and knocked on Necla's door on the ground floor. Necla opened the door and the soldier grabbed her arm and dragged her away without a word. There are white plastic chairs outside the door to the building and everyone always sits on them. The chairs are right on the street and everyone watches anyone who drives past or turns up at our tower block in a car. There is another tower block opposite ours. They also have those white plastic chairs standing on the kerb. That means we all look at each other, we all see the same things, and the street is in between us. The soldier pulled Necla into the middle of the street. He still had hold of her arm. Necla stood with the soldier in the street between the plastic chairs, and everyone sitting on the plastic chairs saw the soldier and Necla. The soldier said, She's one of you but she works for us. You've got a traitor in your ranks. And there are so many of them that you don't even know how many there really are. Necla has pitch-black hair. Hasso used to have black hair too, back when he still had hair. I have white hair and I wear it in a tight plait at the nape of my neck. Necla was beaten, but

Hasso would have died if he had seen. Ayten came running and helped Necla up.

We are stuck in this awful tower block but I want to go home. What are my sons doing? They've been wearing the same clothes for years because there are no clocks in prison. I sew shirts for them; I send the shirts to my sons but they never arrive. Who is intercepting my packages? Who is wearing my children's shirts, with no knowledge of the tower block where Hasso and I sit waiting? I write letters to my sons but only one of my sons answers me. Are my two other sons suffering more than he is? I hope not, I always say.

Sometimes Hasso stands in the doorframe without a door, lies down on the floor, tucks his legs up and goes to sleep. All he's doing is lying under a doorless doorframe and sleeping, but it's the only place he feels safe. Then I lay a blanket over him carefully, so he doesn't get cold. Sometimes it wakes him up and he thinks I'm trying to attack him. Then I say, Hasso, it's me, Nurten. When Hasso forgets where he is and remembers the torture, I can't do anything to stop it. I feel the noose they hung around his neck – for fun, they said, for fun, as if Hasso's life was a made-up story.

My life's made-up too; I count for nothing in this country, I rage against it – write that down – but you get tired of fighting. Now I'm sitting cross legged with floury hands on the floor of our doorless flat. I see policemen throw my Hasso to the floor and pin his arms behind his back. It's a mystery to me. I think of the future, but Hasso and me, all we can do is wait for the future here.

One of the policemen asks, Are you a traitor too?

He says it to my Hasso, not to me. He has a gun in his belt. I used to have a Bixi, it was a good little gun, to protect my animals from poachers. I stand up and say, Please take me with you. I don't ask why they want to take Hasso away. I don't even think about it.

Take me with you. Not my Hasso, he's already been to prison.

When the police hear the word prison, they think Hasso is a wanted man. But Hasso was tortured even though he'd done nothing wrong. Traitors are hanged because they're traitors. They're always men, and it's only men who do it that way. They put a rope around Hasso's neck for fun; it was December, it didn't last long. Please, that's my husband, Hasso, I almost scream, though I don't actually scream. But the policemen drag him through the only door in the house. Above the front door to this doorless flat hangs a picture of our four sons.

That's the future, I say and point to the picture.

But they're already out the door. I drop everything. That's my Hasso, he's done nothing wrong, I cry out in the stairwell and try to run after the four policemen, who are carrying Hasso down the stairs by his arms and legs.

16:11

EPISODE FOUR: BİRGÜL

Birgül lives on the fourth floor. Birgül is named
after her mother's mother. Birgül plays with the
other children in the smallest room of one of
the flats. Birgül doesn't want to stay here.

I've forgotten. I've forgotten where she was sitting. I remember
her legs, pressed to her chest as she sat on the floor. She was
crying. I could see that from where I was sitting. I remember
that well. It wasn't her brother she was crying for, no, it was her
cousin, but I've forgotten where she was sitting. She was sitting
on the floor. It was dark blue, the carpet, I was a child then
but her tears were very real to me. I was eight or nine, maybe,
but I could have been older. I can't remember who it was that
opened the door for us. I didn't hear a ring, didn't see a door
opening, I was just standing in the flat and before I knew it
the door was closed again. I can't remember how late it was.
This all might seem insignificant, it might seem uninteresting.
But it's very important to me.

I stood in the hallway and counted the rooms that led from the
hallway. It was a flat with lots of rooms, though it was narrow.
On the wall on the left was a coat rack, where my jacket was
already hanging. It was ridiculous, I hadn't even taken it off.
On the right, pictures of children hung on the wall. There
were three children in the pictures, but one of them was dead.
In another room, someone said, What does the future hold?
This country is devouring our children. I stood in the hallway;
no one noticed me. I was definitely standing there, in this flat

with its many rooms, with my shoes on the dark-blue carpet, but I wasn't wondering where my parents were. What I mean is: I wasn't part of the family. I was a friend of the family. My parents were both in prison. My mother's friend was looking after me.

My mother's friend was called Ayten. We lived somewhere else before we ended up in the tower block. Like everyone we know. It was in this other place that the boy in the photo died. We didn't know much about the boy's death. Ayten told me later, It was a policeman. There are lots of policemen who could shoot you here.

There were curfews and we weren't actually allowed to leave the house. But Ayten and I did it anyway. We got into a car, but not the way normal people get into cars. We had to lie in the boot. First Ayten got inside and tucked her legs up to leave room for me. Someone grabbed me from behind and lay me on top of Ayten. It was very cramped and I thought we might suffocate. Me first. Then Ayten. But before that could happen, we were suddenly in the flat with all the rooms. Ayten walked through the door and immediately started to cry. When I hear Ayten crying, something insight me tightens.

I stood there motionless and looked at all the people in all the rooms. They were standing side by side in groups and holding hands. Most of the hands were old. It was during the week, not at the weekend. I was sure because I wasn't at school. I scanned all the rooms for the child's mother. I can't remember which room I found her in. The way I remember it, she wasn't in the flat at all. Perhaps she waited in the car until it was all over. Maybe she left the flat with all the rooms and no one noticed?

Not even me, even though I was standing in the middle of the hallway with my back to the door the whole time. But if she just walked out of the flat with all the rooms, when did she come back?

The girl who was crying about her cousin was sitting on the floor. Her hair was long and brown. She either had a centre parting or a hairband on. If it was a hairband, then it was white. She was wearing jeans, I think, and I was still standing in the middle of the hallway, so I walked right over to her, even though the others were crying too. I knelt down on the floor even though she was taller than me. I sat next to her, put my arm around her, cuddled up to her. The way I remember it, she slowly turned her upper body to face me and squeezed my arm with her left hand. It hurt a bit, but I said nothing. Her tears landed on my back. I didn't cry, I'm still sure of that. But I can't remember why I didn't. The girl said my name over and over. I wiped her tears off my face. I can't tell if it really happened. I know for sure that she said my name. I went to her because all the people in all the rooms were crying and she was crying all alone on the floor in the hallway. It was a very long time ago, but I still think about her sometimes. We sat with our backs against the wall. Above us was a picture of a boy, the same age as me. He wasn't dead, his brother was. The brother of the boy in the picture was nine years older. The girl was sitting on the left of the hallway. The left. Yes, I'm quite sure.

Her uncle said, You've got to drink something. Please drink something.
No, she said. No.
He said it again, Please drink something.
He added, For me.

She said, What happened?

I stood in the corner of a square-shaped room with a big bed
in it. On the lefthand side was an old long cabinet, it was grey.
The man with the tea was sitting on a dark-blue sofa and the
woman who didn't know what had happened was sitting next
to him. She wasn't really a woman, she was still a girl. I couldn't
see her because she had wrapped a brown blanket around her
body. I could make out the outline of her body under the
blanket; she was sitting in the same position as the girl on the
floor in the hallway, rocking back and forth. I can't remember
if she was crying out loud. I think she was. It seemed plau-
sible to me that both girls – one on the floor, one under a
blanket – were crying in the same position. They were cousins
too. And because I grew up with them, I would say, These are
my cousins. This habit of sitting to cry must have run in the
family. Now and then I'd see a flash of her white-blue slippers
under the blanket. I'm not sure about the slippers though. I
have a pair of them myself in exactly the same colours. Maybe
I'm getting them muddled. I saw the girl under the blanket
for the first time when the man with the tea pulled the blanket
away from her head.

What happened, she said again.

I was confused by what she was saying because she was repeating herself. She had a tissue in her right hand. What had
happened? Her hair was dark brown. She was wearing a black
polo neck jumper and jeans, I think. The way I remember
it, she didn't get up. The way I remember it, she sat there on
that sofa the whole time. In the first room on the right of the
hallway. Her name was on the door. It read: *Cansu.* Why was

her name on the door? How many people were there in that room? It wasn't just the three of us. I stood right at the back, in the corner so that no one would notice me, so there were definitely other people standing in front of me; otherwise, the man with the tea would have told me to go and play. Cansu's father was standing in the hallway. His name was Haydar. And Haydar was staring into his daughter's room with big, round eyes. He stood across from me and said:

There's nothing to see here.
Then Haydar just collapsed.

The next day, another uncle appeared and brought some baby rabbits to show me and the boy from all the photos in the hallway of the flat with all the rooms. It was a big cage with lots of hay and lots of baby rabbits hopping around. The uncle took one out and said, Here, be very gentle. We stroked it and said, Very gentle. The uncle with the dark brown hair said, Only one each. We nodded but we couldn't decide that quickly because we thought all the baby rabbits were cute. Eventually, he got impatient and we, the boy from the photos and I, we reached down through the grille and into the cage. I was scared because they flinched away from my hand and the impatient uncle with the baby rabbits got even more impatient. He reached into the cage and pulled out two baby rabbits, one at a time. I got a white and brown rabbit. It made me a bit sad because I didn't want a white and brown rabbit. But the impatient uncle wanted us to be happy with the baby rabbits. Don't get me wrong, but I can't remember which rabbit the boy from the photos got.

I asked him, Are you sad about your brother?

He answered, My brother is sick but they took him to hospital in an aeroplane.

His father Haydar heard this and he took me to one side and knelt on the floor in front of me. He put his hands on my shoulders and squeezed a bit too hard, it hurt, but his eyes were big and round again, like the day before, when he'd stood in the hallway and suddenly collapsed, and we were standing in a hallway again when he squeezed my shoulders. He sounded like a wounded man from behind doors in never-ending rooms. It's me, he said. But I knew who it was. Then for a moment I was worried that he was going to collapse again, right in front of me this time. Haydar said quietly, He mustn't remember this. Was this a punishment for me or was it a punishment for his son? Then I looked at the floor. First I felt sorry for Haydar, then for his son.

The next day was the funeral. The funeral was held in a wedding hall. I didn't understand why, so I asked Ayten, who said, Maybe they'll leave us be here. The wedding hall also had lots of rooms. I walked around on my own at first. There was a cloakroom, lots of little toilets, even a shower, two rooms at the back of the corridor on the right and a courtyard. On the wall in the biggest room was a picture of the boy who had died. It was the same picture that had been hanging in the hallway of the flat with all the rooms. The child's mother, who I hadn't seen arrive at the flat, was standing alone in the bathroom of the wedding hall. She was wearing a dress. It was November. The dress was strappy, it went down to her knees. And I thought, if anyone were to find us here, she could pass for a wedding guest. Then she collapsed in front of me. Like Haydar had done. It really frightened me and I called for Ayten. Then it occurred to me that all the funeral guests looked like they were going to a wedding. Ayten was wearing a red dress and she helped the child's mother up and said, I wish I could carry the weight of this with you.

I like Ayten very much. She takes good care of me. I wasn't born in the tower block where we live now. Ayten cut my cord and held my mother's hand when she was having contractions. The two of them were like peas in a pod. My mother's name is Pınar. My name is Birgül and I was named after my mother's mother. My mother was arrested three weeks after I was born. My mother said to Ayten, Take good care of her. After that, Ayten would say I was her child. My mother was put in prison.

Ayten took me with her everywhere because I wasn't her child, I was her friend's. She was constantly afraid that something would happen to me. And since I was her friend's child and not hers, she was even more frightened that harm would come to me. If someone tried to tease me, Ayten would smile and say, No. Of course, the soldiers who were stationed near Ayten's in the city noticed that Ayten suddenly had a baby even though she'd never been pregnant.

A soldier asked Ayten, Where's the child's father?
Ayten replied, He left me.
The soldier said, Who've you been knocking around with, slut?
Then he hit Ayten and Ayten put her arms around me and turned her back to the soldier. She screamed:
THERE'S A TINY BABY IN MY ARMS – WHERE'S YOUR HUMANITY?

He hit her across the back with his gun and replied, That's a terrorist's child, I can smell it from here. Then he stopped and said, Fuck off, I'm sick of the sight of you.

It's common for people to mourn their dead behind closed doors. Sometimes the children will be sent to the smallest room. They're expected to play there and they're not allowed to come out. Every thirty to forty minutes, one of the adults will open the door and look in on them. Their faces will usually be contorted when they open the door to the room. Tearstained. But they don't admit that they've been crying; they wipe their tears away before they open the door. When they open the door to the room, the children go quiet. We soon pick up that there are dead loved ones to mourn. But all the adults do is turn up half an hour later with a plate of fruit cut into small pieces and ask, Are you playing nicely? The children smile and the adults stand in the middle of the room with the plate of fruit in their hands. The lightbulbs are always very dark so it almost always feels like evening. The adults weep for their dead, but not just in the evening – no, in the daytime too. The plate of fruit will be placed somewhere in the room, usually on the floor, because we normally sit on the floor and play. Then the adults will leave the room and close the door again. When they go, they leave as quietly as they came; then the misery they brought into the room clings to us. We sit with the misery because it doesn't go away. We might be in another room but we fall just as quiet as they do. And then it will be a few minutes since the adult left the room and one of the children will say, I'm bored. Even though someone has died. Then we'll go back to playing.

When I'm in my room, I always think of the little rooms in flats where the children end up. Maybe the adults think we'll be safe there from the pain they want to hide from us. But everything they go through they pass onto us, even if they don't tell us about it. From the window in my room, I watched the girl who'd been sitting on the floor of the flat with all the rooms. A man had her hair in his hand and an arm around her waist and was dragging her along the floor. I didn't hear her cry but I saw her thrashing her legs about, trying to escape his grasp. It's a hopeless feeling, being trapped. It's like the smallest room, where all the children end up. I keep very quiet behind the window in my little room. The man is bigger and stronger than the girl, he sits on her, I'm a bit scared that he'll squash her, but he doesn't, he spits in her face. Then he takes his fist and punches her in the nose over and over. I breathe ever so quietly as she bleeds. I watch the blood running down her chin and onto her neck. The man stands up and grabs the girl by the hair again. This time, he simply drags her around the floor. This time she doesn't thrash; she tries to get up.

I turn away from the window and open the bedroom door into the silent flat with no one inside. I put my shoes on and open the front door, then I go down the steps from the fourth floor to the third. I ring the neighbour's doorbell. But no one answers. Maybe they think it's the police at the door, but I'm not the police. The police don't ring the doorbell either. They come straight in through the door or the window. Everyone carries this weight and I sit in endless rooms, waiting until the adults have finished crying. When they're done crying, I open another door into these flats with endless rooms and on the walls there are pictures of children who have been buried. Someone will come out of a room and say, This doesn't leave this flat. And then someone will reply from another room, Close the door behind you.

I stand in the stairwell and look down; the girl from the hall-way, she's on her feet again. I take a deep breath. Then I see a police car I haven't seen before. Then I see the man who spits and hits opening the car door and taking a small bag out of the boot. In the small bag is a small gun, and the man points this gun in broad daylight at the girl with all the rooms. I yell something and the man yells:

YOU PEOPLE STEAL FROM US THEN YOU SHARE IT OUT. BUT WHEN WE STEAL FROM YOU, YOU WON'T GET IT BACK.

And the girl falls to the floor. Write this down: it wasn't even close to nightfall.

02:45

EPISODE FIVE: SARA

Sara lives on the seventh floor. Sara is not afraid of men.
Sara loves her friend Hêlîn. Sara doesn't want to stay here.

WE PUT STONES IN OUR BOOTS
TO MAKE US WALK DIFFERENTLY
BECAUSE A HEAVY TREAD
CAN'T GIVE YOU AWAY
WE SMASHED OUR HANDS AGAINST ROCKS
SO THEY SWELLED UP AND
NO LONGER LOOKED
LIKE HANDS THAT COULD BETRAY US

HANDS CAN ALWAYS EXPOSE YOU
AND OUR HANDS WOULD HAVE REVEALED
THAT WE ARE NOT MEN

NO

WE ARE WOMEN
DRESSED AS MEN
PLAYING SOLDIERS

I GOT US A GUN
YOU CAN BORROW THEM
BUY OR STEAL
I'M GOOD AT IT BUT
ANYONE WHO SPOTTED ME
WOULD HAVE REALISED WHAT WAS MISSING

I HAVE DRY HANDS
GRUBBY HANDS
LIKE A TANK AND A CAR
A TANK IS CAMOUFLAGED
BUT I'M COVERED IN BRUISES

GREEN
BLUE
PURPLE

BECAUSE I SLEEP OUT IN THE BUSHES
IN THE OPEN AIR
AND I SLEEP OUT IN THE BUSHES
BECAUSE I'M HIDING
I'M DOING IT
BECAUSE I RAN AWAY
AND I'M TELLING YOU
LISTEN CLOSELY NOW
NOT EVERYTHING CAN BE UNDONE:

BUT

I WILL RETURN TO THAT PLACE
WE WILL GO HOME AGAIN
AND NO ONE WILL STOP US
MY NAME IS SARA
MY FRIEND'S NAME IS HELIN

EVERY COMMANDING OFFICER
EVERY SOLDIER SPY POLICEMAN
NO MATTER HOW LOW HIS RANK, I'LL
GOD DAMN THEM ALL

I DON'T EVEN BELIEVE IN GOD
WHAT DO I BELIEVE IN
NOT IN THIS COUNTRY

BUT I HOPE GOD VISITS THEM
RIGHT AT HOME
AND CURSES THEM

I WILL HIT BACK
WHEN THEY TOUCH ME
WITH MY HANDS
YES, MY GRUBBY HANDS
DON'T FORGET WHAT I'VE SAID
YES
WRITE THIS DOWN
I TOLD
MY FRIEND HELÎN THIS TOO:

AS A WOMAN, YOU HAVE TO SAVE YOUR OWN LIFE

AND ANYTHING THAT HELPS YOU DO THAT
IS VITAL
IT DOESN'T MATTER HOW YOU DO IT
HELÎN AND I
WE'VE PUT ON UNIFORMS

FIRST THE TROUSERS
THEN THE BOOTS
THEN THE JACKETS

I CUT MY HAIR FIRST
AND THEN IT WAS HELÎN'S TURN

SOLDIERS HAVE SHAVED HEADS

HELÎN HAD LOVELY THICK LOCKS
WHEN I LAY MY HAND ON HER HEAD
HELÎN WAS QUIET AND
WE PUT BERETS ON

THEY COME AT NIGHT
AND SET FIRE TO OUR HAY
IT DOESN'T TAKE MUCH
A CIGARETTE WILL DO IT
IDENTIFY TARGET
AND TAKE AIM
AND STRIKE
THE CIGARETTE LANDS IN THE HAY
IT BLAZES
AND BLAZES
UNTIL IT BURNS DOWN

IT DOESN'T RAIN OFTEN HERE
THE SUMMERS ARE DRY
THE WINTERS ARE COLD
UP IN THE MOUNTAINS THERE IS
SNOW, EVEN IN SUMMER

IN THE DAYTIME WE STACK THE HAY
WE USE THE HAY TO FEED OUR ANIMALS
WHEN THE SOLDIERS COME
WE'RE ASLEEP
WHEN THE HAY BURNS
WE'RE ASLEEP

THE NEXT DAY
THE ANIMALS HAVE NOTHING TO EAT
AND WHEN THE ANIMALS HAVE NOTHING TO EAT
WE HAVE TO SLAUGHTER THEM
WE SLAUGHTER
SHEEP LAMB GOAT
AND THEN WE SHARE IT OUT
SHEEP LAMB GOAT
AND EVERYONE HAS SOMETHING TO EAT

IF WE DON'T SHARE IT OUT
THE MEAT GOES BAD
AND ROTS
AND WHEN MEAT GOES BAD
AND ROTS
WE HAVE TO THROW IT AWAY

THAT MEANS:

WE SHARE IT OUT AND
EAT THE SCRAPS
IT'S ENOUGH FOR ALL OF US
WE HAVE OUR FILL
SO IT'S ENOUGH FOR A WHILE
BUT NOT FOREVER
WE EAT AND THEN THAT'S IT
WHEN WE HAVE NO ANIMALS LEFT
WE HAVE NO MILK NO BUTTER
AND NO CHEESE
EVENTUALLY NO MEAT

WHEN THE HAY BURNS

IT HAPPENS ON PURPOSE
BEFORE A PURPOSE COMES A PLAN
AND BEFORE A PLAN THERE'S A COMMANDING OFFICER
WHO POINTS TO A PLACE AND SAYS:

THERE

THE COMMANDING OFFICER SITS AND WAITS
AND THE SOLDIERS RUN OFF
THAT PLACE BEGINS WHERE OUR LIVES ARE
THAT PLACE TARGETS THE LIVES WE HAVE
IT'S A TRIED AND TESTED TACTIC OF WAR
BUT IT DOESN'T ALL HAPPEN AT ONCE

AND IF THEY HAVE CAPTIVES
THEY WAIT UNTIL IT'S DARK
THEY DON'T COVER THE MEN'S EYES

I'VE SEEN IT MYSELF:

MEN POSITIONED
SIDE BY SIDE
STANDING IN A ROW
SHOT DOWN ONE BY ONE
BEFORE IT WAS THEIR TURN
THEY SAW WHAT THEY WOULD FACE
AS THE NEXT MAN
FELL TO THE GROUND WITH A SHOT TO THE HEAD

I AM NOT AFRAID OF MEN

THEY THINK THEIR FLAG IS A CALLING
WE DON'T FLY THEIR FLAG
THEY ARE WHAT THEY ARE, THEY SAY:

YOU HAVE TO BE SLAUGHTERED

YES THAT'S HOW MUCH WE WEIGH
THAT'S HOW MUCH IT'S ALL WORTH
DEPENDING ON HOW MUCH
THE SOLDIERS CAN CARRY

A LAMB WEIGHS BETWEEN
20
AND
30
KILOS

WE WEIGH MORE

A SOLDIER CARRIES A PACK
PLUS UNIFORM
AND AMMUNITION
THAT'S 25
OR 40 KILOS
ALMOST AS MUCH AS A LAMB

SO THAT MEANS
A SOLDIER IS A LAMB
AND A LAMB IS A SOLDIER
BUT WE'RE NOT LIARS

NO

WE ARE RESIDENTS OF THIS COUNTRY

THEY COME HERE
AND
PILLAGE
LOOT
BEAT

THEN THEY SAY:

YOU ARE TRAITORS TO THIS COUNTRY

EVEN THOUGH THE REAL TRAITORS
ARE UNIFORMED MEN
THE MEN
WHO MARCH THROUGH THE STREETS
WITH BOOTS BELTS AND BERETS
NO MATTER HOW COLD OR HOT
OR WHAT DAY IT IS
BUT YOU KNOW
NONE OF US BELIEVE IT
AND PEOPLE WHO'VE NEVER BEEN HERE
HAVEN'T SEEN IT

AND EVERYONE LEARNS THAT

THE UNIFORM IS WHAT
MAKES A SOLDIER COMPLETE

AND EVERYONE SAYS:

A UNIFORM MAKES
A MAN A MAN

AND MEN ARE SOLDIERS
THEY'RE APPLAUDED
IN FRONT OF THE TV
AND OUT ON THE STREET
THE CHEER RISES FROM AMONG THEIR RANKS
EVERYONE WATCHING UNDERSTANDS
IN FRONT OF THE TV AND OUT ON THE STREET
IN THEIR COUNTRY
THEY MARCH IN THEIR COUNTRY
THEY WALK ALONG THE BORDER HERE
FROM THE OUTSIDE AND FROM THE INSIDE

YET THEY'RE STILL THE SAME
HONOURED CITIZENS OF THIS COUNTRY
BECAUSE THEY UNDERSTAND
MORE THAN EVER
MORE THAN ANYONE ELSE
WHAT IT MEANS
TO BE A CITIZEN OF THIS COUNTRY

THEY SAY:

HE WHO PROTECTS HIS COUNTRY HONOURS IT

AND THE SOLDIER WHO GIVES HIS LIFE
FOR THIS COUNTRY
ON THE BORDER OR IN COMBAT
SACRIFICES HIMSELF FOR HIS COMRADES
FREELY FOR THIS COUNTRY

WILL GO TO HEAVEN FOR EVER
AND EVERYONE WANTS TO GO TO HEAVEN

THEY TELL US:

NO ONE WOULD LOOK FOR YOU IN HEAVEN
THEY'D LOOK FOR YOU WHERE TERROR IS

BUT I'M TELLING YOU
I DETEST THESE MEN
I DON'T WANT HEAVEN IF THEY ARE THERE
IN HEAVEN IT WILL REEK OF THEM
YOU WOULD SMELL IT FROM THE DOORWAY
LET THEM ROT AWAY IN HEAVEN
WITH THE MOON AND THE STARS
BECAUSE I DON'T WANT
TO BE NEAR THEM WHEREVER THEY ARE
I WILL GO BACK HOME

WITHOUT THEM

I WILL NOT LET MYSELF BE
LOCKED UP
BEATEN
OR TOUCHED BY THEM
JUST BECAUSE I'M A WOMAN
THEY HAVE NO RIGHT TO TOUCH ME
BECAUSE THEY REMAIN THE MEN IN THIS
COUNTRY
THEY HAVE NO RIGHT TO TOUCH ME

THEY SAY:

IF YOU LOVE THIS COUNTRY
YOU HAVE NOTHING TO LOSE

THEN THEY SHOOT AT US
FROM BEHIND, THEY SAY:

THIS IS WHAT TERROR IS DOING TO OUR COUNTRY

BUT THE TERROR IN THIS COUNTRY
IS THE VIOLENCE THEY BRING
VIOLENCE IS A NATIONAL SPORT FOR ALL
IN THIS COUNTRY IT'S FREE
VIOLENCE KEEPS THE SOLDIERS
AND THE BORDERS QUIET
THERE'S NOTHING TO EAT
MORNING NOON AND NIGHT
BUT EVERYTHING ELSE IS HERE

ALWAYS THE SAME WHO CARES

THEN THEY SHOOT AT US AGAIN
BUT THEY HUNT PEOPLE BECAUSE THEY SUSPECT
TERROR IN THIS COUNTRY
BEHIND EVERY ROCK
AND IN EVERY ONE OF US

BUT YOU KNOW

IN MY EYES THE LOVE FOR ONE'S COUNTRY
IS THE UGLIEST LOVE
BY THAT I MEAN

THE WEAKEST LOVE

BUT YOU KNOW IT'S COMPLICATED

THERE ARE SOME OF US
WHO ARE HARD LIKE SOLDIERS TOO
EVEN JOINING THEIR RANKS
GETTING PAID AND BUYING
A ROOF OVER THEIR HEADS WITH THE CASH

BUT I ALWAYS SAY:

WHO NEEDS A ROOF OVER THEIR HEAD
OR A FATHERLAND
ALL WE NEED IS
TO BE LEFT IN PEACE

OUR HOUSE NO LONGER HAS A ROOF BUT
IN FRONT OF OUR HOUSE IS A RIVER
THE RIVER COMES OUT OF THE MOUNTAINS
AND FLOWS DOWN TO US IN THE CITY
THE WATER IS COLD
IT'S COLD IN SUMMER
AND IN WINTER
THE SOLDIERS SAID:

THE WATER IS COLD, SARA
YOU'LL FREEZE TO DEATH, SARA
AND IF YOU DON'T FREEZE TO DEATH, SARA
IT'LL BE EVEN WORSE
YOU'LL SMASH INTO A ROCK IN THE WHIRLPOOL
SARA, COME BACK TO LAND

YOU'LL BE SAFE HERE

HELÎN AND I JUMPED INTO THE WATER
FROM HIGH ABOVE
WE STOOD ON A ROCK
AND THE ROCK
WAS ON A MOUNTAIN
AND THE MOUNTAIN LAY

BETWEEN

A CITY AND THIS RIVER
AND BENEATH US THERE WAS NOTHING
BUT THE FLOW
HELÎN AND I
WE HELD HANDS

YES
GRUBBY OR NOT, IT DIDN'T MATTER
THAT'S HOW WE ESCAPED THE SOLDIERS

THEY IMPOSED A CURFEW
THE EVENING BEFORE
IT COVERED HALF THE COUNTRY
ANYONE WHO IGNORED IT
WAS TAKEN AWAY

IN THE FLOW WE WERE
TOSSED BACK AND FORTH
IT WAS NIGHTTIME
IT WAS MISTY
NIGHT AND MIST

I TRIED TO FIND HELÎN

THE WATER LASHED
MY EYES
AND MY NOSE
I HELD MY BREATH
TO KEEP FROM SWALLOWING WATER
THEN I RAN OUT OF AIR
AND HAD TO BREATHE IN
I HAVE NO IDEA
HOW LONG IT WENT ON
AT SOME POINT I WAS WASHED UP
SOMEWHERE ON LAND
OUT OF THE WATER AT LAST

IT FELT LIKE
FIVE WEEKS UNDER WATER
MY FINGERS WERE SHRIVELED
A BIT BLOODIED A FEW SCRAPES
I REMEMBERED HELÎN
I RAN ALONG THE BANK
BUT I DIDN'T KNOW WHERE
I SHOULD LOOK
A FEW DAYS LATER
WE FOUND EACH OTHER
IT WAS A GOOD MOMENT
WE KEPT RUNNING
OUR CLOTHES BEGAN TO SMELL

WET

DRY AGAIN

WET AGAIN

AT NIGHT WE HAD
DRY COUGHS AND WE FROZE
WE DIDN'T KNOW HOW TO MAKE A FIRE

INSTEAD

WE RUBBED EACH OTHER'S HANDS
SO AT LEAST SOMETHING WOULD HELP
TO KEEP US AWAKE
SOMEONE HAD TO KEEP WATCH AT ALL TIMES

I SAID TO HELÎN

WE DON'T EVEN KNOW
WHAT DAY IT IS TODAY

WEEKS WENT BY LIKE THAT
THEN WE SAW SOLDIERS
THE SOLDIERS WERE BATHING IN THE RIVER
AND HAD TAKEN OFF THEIR CLOTHES
THEY WENT IN
AT FIRST WE DIDN'T DARE
BECAUSE NEXT TO THEIR CLOTHES
WERE THEIR GUNS
AND WE THOUGHT

THEY'RE FASTER THAN US
THEY'LL RUN STRAIGHT OUT OF THE RIVER
AND NAKED OR NOT

THEY'LL SHOOT US ON THE SPOT
THERE WERE SEVEN SOLDIERS IN THE WATER
AND ONLY TWO OF US
HELÎN AND ME

I CREPT OVER AND GRABBED TWO PAIRS OF
TROUSERS
AND TWO JACKETS
TWO PAIRS OF BOOTS
AND TWO GUNS

AND WHEN I GOT
BACK TO HELÎN
WE RACED OFF
WE AGREED

TO RUN FOR AT LEAST 45 MINUTES

SO THAT THE DISTANCE WAS GREAT ENOUGH
IN CASE THEY NOTICED TOO SOON

ONLY WHEN 45 MINUTES HAD PASSED
DID WE CHANGE OUR CLOTHES
ONLY WHEN 45 MINUTES HAD PASSED DID WE
NOTICE
THE BOOTS WERE HEAVY AND STANK

BUT THEY'RE BETTER THAN OUR PLASTIC SHOES
YES HELÎN REPLIED

IN WENT THE STONES IN WENT OUR FEET
THERE WERE EVEN SOCKS IN THE BOOTS

SOLDIERS ARE NEAT AND OBEDIENT
AS YOU'D EXPECT
AND HELÎN AND I
WE WERE GLAD OF THE SOCKS
THAT EVENING WAS THE FIRST IN WEEKS
THAT WE DIDN'T FREEZE

HELÎN AND I
WE COME FROM A CITY
WHERE THE TIGRIS FLOWS

THEY HOPED TO CLEANSE OUR CITY
METRE BY METRE
THE POLICE THE ARMY
YES EVERYONE KNOWS THEM
COMMANDING OFFICER AND BATALLION

WE STRUCK OUT
FROM THE EAST
HEADED NORTH

ON THE WAY TO OUR FRIENDS
WE HOPED TO FIND PEACE THERE
BUT WE COULDN'T ESCAPE WHAT WAS HAPPENING
WE GOT CAUGHT UP IN IT AGAIN
IT WAS THE SAME EVERYWHERE
AND WE WERE TOO LATE
OUR FRIENDS WERE NO LONGER THERE

OUR FRIENDS SAID
POLICEMEN ARE MURDERERS

OUR FRIENDS WERE TAKEN AWAY
AND MARCHED TO THE POLICE STATION
FIGHTER BOMBERS AND BATTLE TANKS
COME FROM RUSSIA AND GERMANY
BUT MURDERERS COME FROM THIS COUNTRY
WE CAME FROM THE EAST
AND THERE WERE MORE SOLDIERS THERE
THAN RESIDENTS OF THE CITY

WHEN A SOLDIER IS WOUNDED
THEY TAKE HIM TO THE DOCTOR
OR THEY CARRY THE INJURED MAN
THE WAY COMRADES DO
TOGETHER AS A UNIT
TO A HELICOPTER
BECAUSE NO SOLDIER IS LEFT BEHIND
THE SQUAD MEANS SAFETY
BUT ONLY FOR THEM
HELICOPTERS FLY INTO THE MOUNTAINS
BUT ONLY FOR THEM
IF THERE ARE CASUALTIES
IN THEIR RANKS UP IN THE MOUNTAINS

IF WE'RE DEAD ALREADY
THEY LEAVE US LYING IN THE MOUNTAINS
THAT'S JUST HOW IT GOES
OR THEY PUT US IN A HELICOPTER
IF WE'RE ALREADY DEAD
FLY UP INTO THE MOUNTAINS
SO UP THERE IN THE AIR
THEY CAN THROW US OUT ONTO THE
MOUNTAINTOPS

IT HAPPENS ALL THE TIME

IF NO ONE IS UP THERE
THEN NO DEAD BODIES ARE FOUND
AND IF DEAD BODIES ARE FOUND
NO ONE SEES THEM
BY THEN IT'S MUCH TOO LATE

IN THOSE DAYS EVERY IDIOT WAS ARMED
AND AT THAT TIME
THE SOLDIERS IN THIS COUNTRY
HAD THEIR OWN STORY AND IT WENT LIKE THIS:

ANYONE WHO COMES FROM THE MOUNTAINS
IS A TERRORIST
IF A SOLDIER COMES TO TOWN
HE COMES TO TOWN
TO GO INTO THE MOUNTAINS

DO YOU FOLLOW ME?
YOU COULD NO LONGER TELL
FOES FROM FRIENDS
LOCALS
SPIES
AGENTS
TERRORISTS
SOLDIERS
POLICE
VILLAGE WATCHMEN
CHILDREN
THOUGH THEY COULD BE SPIES TOO

DON'T TALK TO ANYONE
HELÎN'S MOTHER SAID ON THE PHONE

IT STARTED WHEN IT GOT DARK
EVERYONE WAS DEFENDING THEMSELVES

IT SOON WENT WRONG
THAT'S HOW IT ALWAYS GOES
IT DOES NOW AND IT DID THEN

YOU CAN'T SEE A THING
WHEN YOU TAKE AIM IN THE DARK
AND YOU CAN'T SEE
WHO YOU'RE SHOOTING AT EITHER

SOMETIMES SOLDIERS SHOOT AT ANIMALS
SO THEY CAN SAY:

COMMANDER
I'VE BEEN HUNTING TERRORISTS
COMMANDER

THEY'RE BEATEN
IF THEY DON'T SHOOT
THEY'RE BEATEN
IF THEY MISS
IN THE DARK OR IN BATTLE
WE CAN'T TELL
WHICH BULLET OR
WHICH OF THEM
HAS HIT US

ONE NIGHT SOMEONE CAME AND SKULKED
AROUND OUTSIDE OUR HOUSE
WE THOUGHT THE SOLDIERS WERE COMING
TO STORM OUR HOMES

I PICKED UP A GUN
AND WALKED SLOWLY TO THE DOOR
I THOUGHT
IF THEY KICK THE DOOR DOWN
I'LL SHOOT THEM
I HAVE A RIGHT TO
DEFEND MYSELF
I HAVE A RIGHT TO
A PEACEFUL LIFE

EVERYONE IN THIS COUNTRY DESERVES AS MUCH
EXCEPT US

THEN I CREPT ON TOWARDS THE DOOR
THROUGH THE WINDOW I SAW NO ONE
AT SOME POINT HELÎN WHISPERED

THERE'S A SOLDIER OUT THERE
LET HIM COME I REPLIED

WOMEN CAN DEFEND THEMSELVES
WHETHER YOU BELIEVE IT OR NOT
I DON'T CARE
WE HAVE TO DEFEND OURSELVES

THEN I WRENCHED THE DOOR OPEN
FIRED A FEW SHOTS INTO THE AIR

AND THE SOLDIER STOOD
STOCK-STILL WITH FEAR
BECAUSE HE PROBABLY THOUGHT
WE WERE TERRORISTS
NOT COMING FROM THE MOUNTAINS

NO

COMING FROM INSIDE THE COUNTRY
COMING OUT OF HOMES

THEN I HIT THE SOLDIER
ONCE WITH THE GUN
IN THE FACE

HE SAID:

YOU'LL PAY FOR THAT

I SAID:

THERE'S NO ONE COMING IN FROM OUTSIDE

I KNOW WHAT SOLDIERS THINK
THEY THINK:
THEY'RE WOMEN
THEY'RE WEAK

BUT I'M TELLING YOU
WE'RE NOT WEAK
NO
WE'RE NOT

I'LL SAY IT AGAIN
WE'RE NOT WEAK

IF THEY SEE US ON THE STREET
THEY WHISTLE AT US
MAKE KISSING NOISES

THEY SAY:

HEY GIRLS, WHERE ARE YOU OFF TO?

AND YOU KNOW
I ALWAYS SAY WHAT I THINK
AND IF I SAY SOMETHING
I DON'T THINK THROUGH
I DO FIND IT DISGUSTING
BUT IF I DID SAY SOMETHING
THEN I'D SOON BE
AT THE POLICE STATION
AND I DON'T WANT
THEM TO TOUCH ME
OR GAWP AT ME
THEY'D DEFINITELY DO THAT
AT THE POLICE STATION
NO ONE LISTENS TO YOU THERE
SO EVERY TIME
VERY OFTEN
I SWALLOW
MY ANGER DOWN

YOUR HIPS ARE SO BIG AND BEAUTIFUL
ONE OF THEM SAID

KEEP LOOKING AHEAD, SAID HELÎN

COME AND HAVE MY BABIES
HE SAID AGAIN
KEEP LOOKING AHEAD SAID HELÎN

IT TOOK ALL MY EFFORT
NOT TO LOSE CONTROL
THEIR MOTHERS DON'T KNOW
THE KINDS OF SONS THEY HAVE
THEY KNOW THE PICTURES
FROM THE TV NEWSPAPERS
INTERNET

BUT

WE KNOW THESE PICTURES
FROM OUR OWN LIVES
AND NO ONE WANTS
TO HOLD ONTO THEM

I SHOT INTO THE AIR
TOO MANY TIMES
SO THE SOLDIERS
FIRED INTO THE AIR
FROM THE BARRACKS
MUCH LONGER
AND MORE RAPIDLY THAN ME

THOSE WERE THEIR WARNING SHOTS
THEY WERE MEANT FOR US
THEN THE SOLDIER GOT UP

AND WALKED AWAY AGAIN
AS QUIETLY AS HE CAME

HELÎN CRIED IN THE EVENINGS SOMETIMES
HER TEARS WOULD ROLL AND SHE'D SAY

I DON'T KNOW WHERE WE SHOULD GO
I SAID ANYWHERE BUT HERE

OUR SITUATION MAKES US RUMINATE
WE SAT IN AN EMPTY HOUSE AND
WHEN IT GOT DARK
WE KEPT THE LIGHTS OFF

FOR MANY DAYS
WE HAD NO POWER
OR HOT WATER
THE FIGHTING INTENSIFIED
THEN THE POWER CAME BACK
AND THE WATER
THE FIGHTING INTENSIFIED
IT HAPPENED OUTSIDE OUR FRONT DOOR

THEN THE SOLDIERS CAME
THEY RAVAGED THE CITY
FIRST THEY SET FIRES
IN THE FORESTS
THE FIRE SPREAD
DOWN FROM THE MOUNTAINS
UP TO OUR DOOR
IN THE FORESTS THE ANIMALS DIED FIRST
THEN THE TREES CAME DOWN

A NEIGHBOUR SHE HOLLERED

YOU BASTARD ANIMALS
YOU CAN
SET THE WHOLE WORLD ON FIRE
UNTIL WE BURN TO DEATH
AT LEAST WE'D BURN
WITH GOOD HEARTS
BY OUR OWN FRONT DOORS
BUT YOU'RE BURNING THIS PLACE DOWN
FAR FROM HOME

THE NEXT DAY
THEY HAD GONE
PROBABLY TO THE POLICE STATION
LIKE OUR FRIENDS

THEY CHASED US THROUGH THE STREETS
WITH IRON BARS
THEY PACKED A PUNCH
ONE BAR WAS COLD
ONE BAR WAS WARM

WHEN A SOLDIER DIES
HIS FUNERAL
IS SHOWN ON TV
BUT ONLY NOW AND THEN
TO KEEP MORALE UP
BECAUSE SOLDIERS DON'T DIE
SOLDIERS ARE HEROES

AND THESE HEROES ARE

THE COUNTRY'S SAVIOURS
AND SAVIOURS ARE IMMORTAL
WHICH ALSO BOOSTS MORALE

WHEN A SOLDIER DIES
HIS FUNERAL
IS SHOWN ON TV
WE WATCH IT TOO
THEN A WHOLE NATION WEEPS
FOR ITS HEROES
IN HEAVEN AND ON EARTH
WHEN WE DIE
ONLY OUR MOTHERS WEEP
YOU DON'T SEE THEM ON TV

THEN WE LEFT
SOLDIERS CAME AGAIN AT NIGHT
BARGED INTO OUR FRIEND'S FLAT
ONE SOLDIER GRABBED HELÎN
ONE SOLDIER GRABBED ME
THEY PUT US ON THE BED
NEXT TO EACH OTHER A LITTLE APART
I THOUGHT THEY WOULD RAPE US
BUT THEY STRAIGHTENED OUR CLOTHES
WE COULDN'T DEFEND OURSELVES
WITH OUR ARMS
TWO SOLDIERS STOOD BY OUR HEADS
AND TWO BY OUR FEET

THEN ANOTHER SOLDIER CAME
HE PLACED HIS HAND
ON MY THIGH

I SAID
GET YOUR HAND OFF ME
HE SAID
WE'VE GOT YOU NOW SLUT

HIS HAND ROAMED
UP MY LEG
THEN HIS HAND
WAS UNDER MY DRESS
THEY FORCED HELÎN
TO OPEN HER MOUTH
ONE OF THEM STUCK HIS FINGER INSIDE
SOLDIERS HAVE NOTHING AGAINST VIOLENCE

ON THE CONTRARY

THEY STAPLED OUR CLOTHING
TO OUR BODIES

TACK
TACK
TACK
IT BURNED

WE DIDN'T CRY OUT

I HAD NEVER EXPERIENCED
ANYTHING LIKE IT BEFORE

THEN THEY GAVE US ELECTRIC SHOCKS
FIRST ON THE SOLES OF OUR FEET

THEN IN OUR FACES
DID THEY KNOW
IF IT WAS TORTURE OR NOT
I'M TELLING YOU THEY DID
THAT'S WHY THEY DIDN'T STOP
THEY GET EXTRA MONEY
FOR TORTURE
THERE'S A BONUS
FOR EVERY PERSON TORTURED
THERE'S EXTRA CASH
THERE WERE TWO OF US
HELÎN AND ME
THAT'S DOUBLE THE MONEY
OUR FRIEND'S FLAT
BECAME A PRISON
FOR HELÎN AND ME
AND IT WAS ONLY DAYS LATER
WE MANAGED TO ESCAPE

WE WOUND UP IN THIS TOWER BLOCK
AFTER HEARING THAT THERE WAS
THIS TOWER BLOCK
WHERE EVERYONE WAITED AND SAT
WAITED AND WATCHED
UNTIL SOMEONE CAME
AND THAT PERSON
COULD BE SOMEONE FROM THEIR PAST

IN THE STAIRWELL I SAID OUT LOUD:

IF YOU FORGET WHAT'S HAPPENED
YOU'LL NEVER FIND A SOLUTION

WE TRIED IT ONCE WITH STORIES
AND NOW WE'RE TRYING IT WITHOUT
DON'T GET ME WRONG
THE STORY IS TORN
FROM UNDER MY FEET

LOCALS
SPIES
AGENTS
TERRORISTS
SOLDIERS
POLICE
VILLAGE WATCHMEN
CHILDREN
BUT THEY COULD BE SPIES TOO

AND I'M TELLING YOU:

ANYONE WHO RELATES EVENTS
WITHOUT TELLING STORIES
HASN'T EXPERIENCED THEM
ISN'T BEING GENUINE WITH US
THERE'S NO OTHER EXPLANATION
FOR THESE PICTURES NOW

IT IS WHAT IT IS
AND ANYONE WHO DOESN'T GET THAT
FAILS TO SEE THE PICTURES
WE CAN'T SHAKE OFF
BECAUSE WE HAVE TO ENDURE THEM

THE SOLDIERS SAY:

THERE'S ONLY ONE GOD HERE
AND THAT GOD IS OUR GOD
AND OUR GOD PROTECTS THIS COUNTRY
AGAINST TERRORISTS

BUT I'M TELLING YOU:

IT'S STUFFY IN THIS TOWER BLOCK
UGLY ON THE OUTSIDE
AND UGLY ON THE INSIDE
HELÎN AND I
WE SHARE A ROOM HERE
OUR ROOM IS A SMALL ROOM
A ROOM IN NURTEN'S FLAT
SHE'S A FRIEND OF MY MOTHER'S
HER FLAT HAS NO DOORS
EXCEPT THE DOOR TO OUR ROOM
NURTEN BAKES BREAD AND
HER HUSBAND SITS ON THE FLOOR
WHEN NURTEN BAKES BREAD
WE SIT WITH HER HUSBAND
AND SAY NOTHING

BUT I'M TELLING YOU:

HATE AND PUNISHMENT
LIVE IN THIS TOWER BLOCK
AND WE LIVE AMONG THEM

NO ONE HAS BETRAYED US HERE

BUT IF YOU WALK OUT
IT'S OVER

THEY TOOK OUR FRIENDS
SOMEWHERE ELSE
FROM THE POLICE STATION
WE'RE IN OUR HIDING PLACE
BUT THE MEN ARE COMING BACK
RIGHT NOW

FOR HASSO

BUT NURTEN WON'T LET HIM GO

HELÎN AND I
WE'RE IN OUR HIDING PLACE
WHEN WE HEAR FOOTSTEPS
OUTSIDE OUR HIDING PLACE
I HOLD HELÎN'S MOUTH SHUT
I PRESS MY LIPS TOGETHER HARD
UNTIL THEY'RE PROBABLY BLUE
LIKE IN THE WATER

UNTIL I STOP BREATHING
WE LIE ON OUR BELLIES

NURTEN SAYS:
MY HUSBAND THAT'S MY HASSO

HELÎN TWITCHES
NURTEN SAYS

THERE'S TWENTY KILOS
OF BREAD DOUGH IN THE FRIDGE
IT'S FOR THE FUTURE

THEN THEY'RE GONE
BUT WE HAVEN'T CHANGED
WE STILL SAY

WE DON'T LOVE
THE FATHERLAND
OR THE NATION

WE SAY THIS
AT LEAST A HUNDRED TIMES A DAY

THEY LOVE THE FATHERLAND
AND THE NATION
EVEN IF THEY SHOOT
THOUGH THEY CAN'T SEE
IN THE DARK

I TAKE MY HAND OFF HELÎN'S MOUTH

THE FIRE BEGINS IN THE MOUNTAINS FIRST
THE ANIMALS DIE
WHEN IT REACHES US THIS TIME
WE ARE IN THE FLATS
AND WE SUFFOCATE HERE

NOW IT'S MY TURN TO STAY AWAKE
AND HELÎN IS GOING TO SLEEP

03:07

EPISODE SIX: UMUT

Umut lives on the fifth floor. Umut talks about police
violence all day long. Umut knows that soldiers fly
Cobra helicopters. Umut doesn't want to stay here.

I live on the fifth floor. This tower block has seventeen floors.
There's one girl living above me on the sixth floor, and there's
another below me on the fourth floor. The girls are cousins.
Well, not really. But the one from the fourth floor, her name is
Birgül, her parents are in prison so Ayten is looking after her.
And because the two girls have known each other their whole
lives, they say, We're cousins. I don't know how old they are.
I've never asked. Maybe thirteen and fifteen. I'm forty-four.
My name is Umut. It took me a long time to suss out their
system. One of them will start jumping in the flat above me,
sometimes it goes on for twenty minutes. Then she jumps on
the spot until I run furious into the kitchen to grab the broom.
My flat is small. Because of the two girls, I'm always walking
from one room to the next, looking for the broom. I've been
very forgetful recently. It took me two years to understand
that this is how the girls communicate. When the girl above
starts jumping and I get the broom and knock on the ceiling,
the girl underneath knows – because she hears me knocking,
the walls are very thin – that her cousin is jumping and has
something to tell her. Then they meet up on the roof. People
are very inventive in times of crisis. It makes me happy. The
telephones in the tower block are tapped, so this is the safest
option for the girls. I can't hold it against them, really. In

hindsight, I feel sorry for being so angry with the two of them. I wish I'd known sooner.

Please don't get me wrong. These days, I can't be sure what happened. And by that I don't mean that the reality we speak of and the violence we experience don't correspond. No, it all fits. In this country, reality only works through violence. I've never seen any different. And that violence ties you to their reality. In every reality there are soldiers, policemen, units that don't trust you. It's the same for us, too. What I mean by that is: we respond to them the way that they respond to us. It makes everyday life harder. The distrust grows. I mean, you don't even get a chance to talk about it. Where are you supposed to begin. You don't even know where the beginning is. It's a crisis the whole country is caught up in. Everyone who lives here, I mean. But not everyone talks about it. Maybe not all of them have something to say about it. Those who live in the West don't tend to be interested in the East at first. Only once they've been here do they say: Everything's different over there. Which means something has happened here. In times of crisis, there are true tears and false tears. Both true and false tears flow from people's eyes, but you can't tell which kind of tears anyone is crying these days.

Here in the tower block, no one leaves their flat in the evenings anymore. You're sure to get arrested if you venture out. There are often soldiers outside our door. Or policemen. Some policemen, for instance, are especially deranged You can tell straight away. They'll grab you on the street and break your arm, just like that. And no one will come to help. They do whatever they want. And you can't go to the police with your injuries, not if it's the police who've hurt you. Do you understand how absurd that is? Here in the tower block, everyone says, They come at night. By that they mean the men. But that doesn't always fit with reality. I always say, If they come at night, they can come in the day too. Policemen or soldiers. Oh, what do I know? Some kind of unit. At the end of the day it doesn't matter who it is. A squad. They're just men. All men. Gendarmeries. Full of men. Whatever. Anti-terror units. So what. The point is, they strike. Explosives, belts, guns. It's lost on me. I don't even want to list this stuff. Explosives, belts, guns. It only makes matters worse. But why should I keep my mouth shut? If you don't talk about things, you can't solve them. Actually I'd much rather be rid of it all. You don't have to drag these things around with you all the time. That's why I'm talking about them now. I'm going to talk about police violence. That's what concerns me the most. My name is Umut. Yes, I said that already. What do they expect from us? The state, I mean. Policemen and soldiers, more than anything. Would they like us to keep our mouths shut until we disappear and then to stay wherever we've disappeared to until we die? When you get disappeared by a special unit, you're taken to an unknown location and beaten. That's what they did to my brother. He was almost beaten to death. I don't want to be beaten to death. People who know about these things have to talk about them. Many people don't know about these things. But it's still important to talk about them. Even if it's forbidden. You can't go to the police. So you avoid uniform men. But they burst into flats morning, noon, and night. When they burst in, we jump out of our seats and put our hands up.

No one jumped in the tower block yesterday. Last night, I was lying in bed and couldn't sleep. It was very late and I kept tossing and turning. Eventually I got up, put on my dressing gown, walked barefoot through the flat in the darkness. How can I describe my flat to you? There's a hallway, a kitchen, a living room, a bedroom, a bathroom. Yes, I know, you're probably not interested in any of this. But it's important to explain these things. I'm constantly comparing my flats in my head. I don't live in my old flat anymore, I live in this new one. I tell myself: Umut, the bedroom in your old flat had four windows. Here you have two. Or I say: Umut, you put a big red rug on the floor in the hallway of your old flat. You don't have one here.

But this is where I live now, and the things I talk about are snapshots of moments with details added in. It's no good just thinking about the future either. In this case, though, I'm thinking about forgetting things from the past. That requires space too. I describe things to distract myself. And sometimes I think the details I'm describing aren't detailed enough. What kind of details? The full sequence of events. But it was dark. I couldn't see anything. What can I tell you? I hadn't done anything wrong. No, I hadn't. A soldier has all sorts of reasons. His reasons are accepted all the way up to the country's borders. And sometimes beyond them too. A soldier gets to know his fatherland and a commanding officer explains the soldier's duties. Then the soldiers explain our duties to us. These duties are orders. I don't want them. I had a house in a different city. There was a chair next to my bed there. It's different here.

Anyway, it was nighttime and I couldn't sleep. Then I heard a scream outside. It was very loud, like a cat being run over by a car. Then I heard the scream again and it was only then that I realised it wasn't a cat but a person. I went out onto the balcony and saw a police car. It was just the one car at first. Then there were more and more of them. There were policemen sitting in each car. But they weren't wearing police uniforms. So they weren't policemen anymore. They were some sort of special unit. But they were still policemen. It's all the same here anyway. There were lots of them. I tried to count them but I can't count. Don't laugh at me. In fact, go on, laugh at me if you want to, I don't care. I earn my money on the street. I sit on the ground and sell tissues. My daughter always used to sit next to me but the men took her away too.

The police charged into our tower block. My balcony is right over the main entrance. It was like a front row seat. They ran inside in a frenzy. Not in an orderly line like they usually would. All the lights went on in the floor above mine. I could only guess that they were heading upstairs because all the windows I could see from my balcony were dark. And it was three o'clock in the morning – or at night, depending on how you look at it. Then someone screamed. I couldn't tell if it was a man or a woman. But this time it didn't sound like a cat; it instantly sounded like a human being. Tower blocks always have lots of people living in them. It's the same here. You can never be sure of how many there are. Everyone who runs away ends up here. Or somewhere else. My brother, for instance, he left the country. What I mean by that is: everyone says that the units come at night, but I'm telling you, nighttime is also when we run. I didn't have the heart to run. My brother did.

He got hold of five thousand euros. That's high-value money. Higher value than our money. He worked hard for it and did the worst jobs. He saved it up in an envelope and he hid the envelope in his room between his mattress and the bedframe. Then he gave his high-value euros to a high-value smuggler who got him papers. Then my brother had to get hold of another five thousand high-value euros so that another high-value smuggler would get him over the border. My brother is younger than me. My brother sang a banned song at a demonstration. Afterwards, a letter arrived at the house and then my brother was landed with a court case. He was reported for treason. They make you serve time for treason. But my brother's not a traitor. He sang the song on the street outside our house. I sang along and clapped my hands. My brother has a very beautiful voice. He didn't want to go to prison; I didn't want him to either, but I also didn't want him to disappear over the border. Eventually, though, that day arrived. We met in a small restaurant off the main road.

My brother was about to leave the country forever but he didn't have a bag with him. When I asked where his things were, he replied: I'm not taking anything with me, it'd attract too much attention. I was worried he would be cold on the long journey. My lentil soup was very hot. But I wasn't hungry. I set the spoon down on the table and examined my brother's thin jacket. Then I started ruminating. I wondered what I would take with me if I was leaving the country at night. I thought: *When you run away, you flee the life you're trying to escape.* What else matters then? Life, perhaps? No, that can't be it. Because that's what you're running from. If I left the country, I'd say I was leaving because of the police.

My brother held my hand and I went with him to meet the smuggler. Where do I start? I can't put it into words. It would be easier to describe losing your mind. Yes, really. Something in your brain burns. And all I can say is: my brother was standing there. What I saw: behind my brother there's a man. What I understood: the man standing behind my brother is the smuggler. What I also noticed: the smuggler is almost as old as my brother. I repeat: my brother is leaving this country for another country but in the other country he'll be far away from me. My brother hugged me for a long time. I took a deep breath and I saw: my brother, the smuggler, the other men with the smuggler. They were all wearing shirts and trousers and thin jackets. My little brother waved at me and I made sure I could see: my brother getting into the smuggler's car. My brother sat by the window. The engine started up.

In our region, this is what it's like: soldiers sitting in Cobra helicopters, firing from the air. Policemen sitting in police cars, firing from the windows. My little brother was sitting in a smuggler's small grey car, trying not to go to prison. Standing there, I was very worried that the smuggler might not be a smuggler at all. That's not uncommon, you know. People give smugglers money and they get papers. Then they get into the smuggler's car and it turns out the smuggler's not a smuggler, he's a spy. From some special unit. The spy doesn't drive to the border. No, the spy drives the passenger straight to prison. The transition from passenger to prisoner goes off without a hitch. God forbid. My brother said, Life goes on. Those were his last words through the window. I'LL WAIT FOR YOU, I shouted after him. It didn't make any sense. He was going away and I was staying behind. So he was the one who'd wait for me somewhere else. The car became smaller and smaller and I said to myself: It just keeps going.

Sometimes you get twenty people living in one flat. They put all the children between two and twenty years of age in one room. Inside, there's nothing but mattresses, blankets, pillows on the floor; they all sleep in one room. We used to do the same. But back then, everyone ran off to different places. My daughter Mira and I, we didn't run. One night, we set off walking. I had a small rucksack and Mira didn't have one because she was very small and I didn't want her carrying anything heavy. I didn't tell Mira we were leaving our home. I didn't want her to be sad. So I took her from her bed one night. I didn't wake her; I carefully carried her out of bed with her head resting on my shoulder. I knew the soldiers would come soon and it was time for us to go. I could hear machine guns and helicopters in the distance. The neighbours were getting restless and putting their furniture out in the street. I didn't do that, so why were they doing it? I didn't know if the soldiers were going to attack us; if they were far away or close by. My Mira lay sleeping in my arms and I stood in the street, not moving.

Then I did something I'll never forget as long as I live. I lay my sleeping child down in the bushes. I went to the barn. I took a can of petrol. The bed, the blankets, the floor, the table – with my own hands, I doused the stuff of my life with petrol. My brother was wearing a thin jacket and had left everything behind. I was doing the same. And I think that's the only reason I managed to escape.

I saw: Mira's toys. Covered in petrol.
I saw: Lentils, aubergines, tomatoes. Covered in petrol.
I saw: Rugs, cushions, TV. Covered in petrol.

I knew: I'm taking these matches and throwing them into the house. Into my house. It was my house.

I even covered every inch of the bathroom in petrol. I was very thorough. Then I ran outside, screaming as I went because I was suddenly aware of what I'd done. I threw maybe a hundred or two hundred burning matches into each room. I even set light to the curtains. The curtains burned very quickly. It didn't take long at all. What I mean by that is: it happened so fast. The fire grew bigger and bigger.

As the house began to burn, Mira was still sleeping in the bushes. As the house burned, I realised that many things are worthless but not useless. It was the second-worst thing I had done in my life. Genuinely. It really took it out of me. And I never would have done it if things hadn't been the way they were. But back then I thought: They won't get me this way. I'll keep my dignity. My conscience helped me sustain that dignity. And, of course, my conscience had to get on with it. But I thought, I'd rather set my house on fire. I'd rather end this with my own hands. I couldn't bear the thought that soldiers might destroy my home and then set it alight. I thought that it would be different if I did it. That I'd retain a final scrap of respect and dignity. It might sound strange to you, but sounding strange doesn't help with the balance of power. The damage they bring to our doors can't just be swept away. The damage is like dirt; it's not just us it sticks to, it sticks to everyone. Inside and outside, you lose all control. What else is there to say when you have to stand in the street and watch what they do?

I went back to Mira; she was still asleep, I picked her up again and walked away. I carried Mira ever so slowly so that she wouldn't wake up. Behind me I could smell the stench of things in the fire. I whispered quietly: See this, Mum, thank God you're not around to see this.

We walked for weeks, Mira and I. Well, it wasn't like we could go to the police. We slept in caves, ate berries and roots. I picked flowers for Mira from the meadow to make her happy. My daughter was very brave. I cried at night when she was asleep. As soon as I fell asleep the nightmares would come, I'd see the smoke rising from our house. I dreamt I was suffocating in the smoke. I dreamt that soldiers doused me in petrol and set me alight. Policemen watched and laughed. They laughed and said, Thought you'd got away, did you? Whenever I woke up screaming, I'd look at Mira and fall silent. I wanted to spare my Mira the worry.

But my daughter is gone now. My daughter looked like me. I'm searching all over for her but I don't know where to start. Like I said, I can't go to the police. Men came after us. That was at nighttime too. I ask you, what do people do in the dark at nighttime when they can't sleep? Yes, that's right. They stay awake.

Everyone says, They come at night.
I always said, Or at the crack of dawn.
And at noon. When it's light, I mean.

But they came to us in the darkness. They didn't knock; they just rammed the door down. I didn't see what they did it with because I was busy telling my daughter to hide under the bed or in the cupboard. Why there, exactly? Because doors can be shut, maybe that's why. The living room door was on the floor in front of me and all I could see was the gun that someone was pointing in my face. Another person pounced on me from behind (how long had they been standing behind me?). I lay on the floor and saw my daughter under the bed looking back at me. It was a quiet moment that I'll never forget. That was the last time I saw her. It's a mystery to me why they took my daughter and not me. I whispered, Mira. Why did I whisper her name? She was lying on the floor not far from me. Why did I whisper her name? Maybe because I was afraid for her. That's probably what gave her away. That really upsets me. I'd rather suffocate with my things in the smoke of my burning house. I'd rather the soldiers doused me in petrol and set me alight. I'd rather the policemen laughed. I had barely uttered her name when a soldier dragged her out from under the bed. My Mira was nine years old.

Back at the tower block someone is screaming again. It's a woman this time. Maybe a mother. Like Mira's mother when she was shot dead in the street by a policeman. I didn't scream when they took my daughter away. I threw up. All down myself. On my shirt and on my trousers. Like a baby spits up. I fainted. When I woke up, the whole flat had been ransacked. The pictures had been torn from the walls; they were lying on the floor like Mira and me. Shards can be swept up. The sofa and the mattresses were slashed open. Why? What was the point in doing that? When a person disappears, the damage is bad enough. It's enough. All the cupboards were wrenched open. Cupboard doors lay scattered across the floor. Clothes had been ripped up. My daughter's books torn in two. The pages had been ripped out, even though they were only school-books. The tap was running in the kitchen. Water was pouring onto the floor, but my daughter was gone. I didn't even have to look for her. I already knew. How did I know? Because I'm a father who loves his daughter. On the wall in the kitchen, next to the tap, they had left me a message.

We'll be back.

That was my only hope. I saw another flat destroyed. But this time my Mira wasn't sleeping in the bushes. My Mira was gone. Like my brother and the smuggler. Where had they gone? I stared at the wall. Why are they all gone? On the opposite wall it said: *Traitors have nowhere to hide.* I turned to the other message and read it again: *We'll be back.* I thought: *If they come back and take me away, I'll find out what happened to my daughter. Or where she is. If I find out where my daughter is, I'll save her.* This simple hope was my only salvation.

Here at the tower block, the same thing happens time and again. There were more and more policemen standing outside the entryway. What I saw: guns in their hands. They were laughing as they dragged a man out of the doorway. Why were they laughing? They always do. I couldn't tell how old the man was. I saw: a policeman's gun aimed at the back of his head. Behind him a woman was trying to get past the policemen to her husband. She didn't vomit like I did. She screamed:

Hasso. Please, that's my husband Hasso.

One of the policemen hit her in the head with his gun. I couldn't see if she was bleeding. But I saw her fall to the ground. Then came another policeman; he gave her a proper kicking. Square in the face, I think. He did it again and again. I saw her white hair on the brown ground. The policeman roared: We'll be back. We'll get you all. I thought, *Please take me.* I thought, *He means me.* My only hope was Mira. I started to cry. Not because of the woman but because of Mira. I feel ashamed about that now. The woman had stopped moving.

The man was weeping and screaming, Nurten, please get up. But Nurten, his wife, just lay there. Her head hung over the steps, she lay on her front and her upper body slid down the steps. I thought she was dead. Why did I think that? Nurten didn't look like a person anymore. But then she started moving. Then she stood up and said: What future is there for us in this country? Then she slumped down again. Was it winter or summer? It was nighttime, that much is certain. My house burned at nighttime, my brother disappeared at nighttime, Mira disappeared at nighttime, it was nighttime when Nurten lay on the entryway steps, and it was nighttime when I stood on the balcony because I couldn't get to sleep.

When you're tortured, the seasons are very important. Without the seasons, time remains something that functions outside of torture, something there's no language for. When you're tortured, you can't escape the torture but sometimes you can escape time with the seasons. Then you think of the season and hide away in springtime. I think of that spring with Mira in the meadow, when I gave her the flowers.

Now the police are ramming the flat door down again. I was sad that I had set fire to my house. Mira was asleep, and it burned. I was outraged that my brother had gone away in the smuggler's car.

Are you taking me to my daughter? I ask weakly.

All I want is to go to Mira. Nothing happens at first. But then. It's over. They're taking me with them, thank God. I'm not standing in front of the car anymore, waiting for my brother. Escaping the burning house. I've never had a carefree life, but

Mira is my carefree season. Thank God they're taking me with them. I don't faint this time and no tears come, true or false. No, this time we'll be different. I'm against police violence but I don't need to tell the police that. They already know.

19:23

EPISODE SEVEN: HAYDAR

Haydar lives on the ninth floor. Haydar sits in a chair in his
room all day, looking out of the window. Haydar doesn't talk
and he doesn't explain. Haydar doesn't want to stay here.

I set out to avenge my son. But what does that even mean?
Revenge can be interpreted in all sorts of ways. My son's name
was Devin. Revenge can right past wrongs. Or perhaps it
can't. My name is Haydar. Devin was shot dead at night-time.
Revenge is both good and bad. Devin has an elder sister and
a younger brother. Revenge doesn't talk and it doesn't explain.
In my wife's flat there were lots of pictures of Devin, framed
on the wall. We don't live together anymore, my wife and I.
We're divorced, my wife and I. When we heard our son had
been killed, we broke down. I fell to the ground first; *Get up,*
my wife told me, but as she said it she collapsed too, then she
was on the floor beside me. No one can tell me exactly how
it happened. There's no way to talk about this tragedy. I don't
want to talk and I don't want to explain. But I don't know the
truth. And stories like these are always the worst in the world.
And all over the world, these stories never come to an end.
Some of our neighbours were at home when it happened. But
they were all asleep. It happened around two in the morning.
It was November. I repeat: the neighbours were all asleep.

The sound of gunshots was what woke them. Once the shots
had startled them awake, it all happened so fast that they
couldn't tell what had woken them up. By the time they were
awake, the noise had already stopped. They fell back to sleep

while my son was still alive, but he was only alive for as long as he was the target. Again, he was shot at and again, it woke the neighbours up.

Who knows what a gun sounds like? I was somewhere else at the time and not with my son, but I know what a gun sounds like. I know because after I fell to the ground and my wife and I lay there together, I got up and I said to my wife:

I'LL KILL HIM.

I had no idea who I wanted to kill or what had even happened.

All I knew was that they had shot my child ten times in total. Four bullets struck him in the chest, three in the neck – it's a small area but you can hit it over and over, you can't imagine it – one went into his right upper arm and one hit him between the knee and the thigh. The tenth bullet didn't hit him, it lodged in the wall behind him. At least he was spared one bullet. At least he was spared that. That meant a lot to me. It might sound unimportant to you – because nine bullets in, it's already too late. But you know, I'm glad that the tenth bullet didn't hit him. Write that down.

The bullets hit him in the chest, neck, upper arm and knee, so we can say with some certainty that the person shooting was not standing very far away from my child.

The opposite of war is not peace. The opposite of peace is torture. The opposite of a good and a bad life is simply death. I paced up and down the room for days, trying to understand and find out what had happened. I didn't tell my other two children anything. I told my younger son that his brother had boarded an aeroplane and that the aeroplane had left the country. The plane had flown to another country because my son, his older brother, was ill. My younger son believed this story. I was astonished, you know; in that moment I had no idea what had got into me. At first I thought: *Oh you stupid child, your brother's dead and you think he's in an aeroplane.* But then I understood. My son has been shot and my younger son doesn't know about it. I was stringing my child along with the story. Or perhaps I was sparing myself the ending. I sent him and his cousin to my brother's; he gave the children a rabbit each. Then my son, his name is Diyar, was standing in the stairwell outside our door in his jeans, which didn't really fit him, holding the animal in his arms and looking at me with wide eyes. We had no money for a cage, so the rabbit lived in a banana box.

I always tried to hide my tears from Diyar. When the tears were unavoidable, I found lies to explain them away. Usually, I said:

The film on TV is a sad film. The film is about a man who doesn't remember his mother even though she's standing in front of him. It's a terrible thing, son.

He nodded, stroked his rabbit and said, That would never happen to me. Diyar was seven years old when my son Devin died. The cardboard box was between the TV and the sofa and Diyar lay on the floor on his belly in front of the TV and the cardboard box, and I sat on the sofa in front of a coffee table, a grey one, watching my son, my living son, with his rabbit in a cardboard box, but my fear kept going round in circles. This is when everything stops, I said. Has the film finished? my living son asked. I said nothing. Then I understood. Everything I've gone through, my children will go through too. Everything my children go through, they'll recognise from their past. It becomes a habit. And a habit becomes a life.

In the weeks that followed, Diyar and I spent all our evenings like this. He'd be busy with his rabbit – which still didn't have a name, we called it *Rabbit* – and I would just sit there on the sofa, stiff, with the TV on in front of me. I didn't even turn it off when I went to sleep at night. The news would be on, reporting on other things. We saw hills, mountains, helicopters. The newsreader's voice said, This is where they were captured. And we couldn't see any people, just a rock that had been blown up. Was my child behind the rock? No, no. My son didn't appear. Every picture was a picture without him. I said, Pictures lie. But everything reminded me of him, so I couldn't stop looking for him. Diyar didn't understand why I kept bursting into tears, even at the weather. He lay his rabbit in my hand and said, *Very gentle.*

Please don't get me wrong; I was sad because I'd lost my child. I didn't know how the catastrophe inside me would spread. It was like being on guard. I would sleep for fifteen minutes. Then I'd wake with a start because I thought someone was kicking the door in, soldiers or policemen, anyone, to attack me, to attack my children, and I couldn't save my two children. I'd start gasping for breath just thinking about it. *Something bad's going to happen,* I thought, and I won't realise it's happening because I'll be asleep. Like the neighbours were that night. I always slept without a blanket, on purpose, to make sure I was a little cold. If you're cold when you sleep, you wake up fast. And if you wake up fast, you can't sleep through anything. Like the neighbours, who didn't hear all those bullets because they were sleeping.

That's why I sit here on the sofa. Usually I don't even lie down, I just sleep sitting up. If my head starts nodding, I jolt awake and look straight into the hallway to check that there's no one in our flat. It's not like anyone could get in: I double lock the door, leave the key in; I've got three reinforced locks which are bolted as soon as we get home – still, you never know, do you. Sometimes, when they come to take someone away, they come through the window and even a thousand locks and bolts won't help. These things don't help anyway, at the end of the day, because they could just ram the door down. When I see there's no one in the hallway, I know that I've just woken up because I've slept for fifteen minutes and my head has nodded to the side.

My wife never sat with us. My wife was always in the bedroom. The curtains were closed in the bedroom. The bed was made. The room was always neat and tidy. Wardrobe. Chest of draw-ers. Two bedside lamps. Two windows. A mirror. And my wife lay there with her legs tucked up on the side of the bed she always slept on. She wore jeans and a jumper. Her chin was cradled in the crook of her right elbow. Days passed us by in this misery. She lay there and I sat next to her on the bed, on the same side she lay on, the same side she always lies on when she goes to sleep at night.

You could well have missed her if you hadn't known she was on the bed. You couldn't even hear her breathing. Sometimes I forgot she was there at all. She was so quiet that on some days

I stood in the hallway and charged over to her, hoicked her up by the armpits – I was a civilian, left behind – and shook her, I didn't want to hurt her but lately I've found myself snapping and losing my head – I didn't mean her any harm, believe me, something just broke out of me, it must have been the lack of sleep or something – and I roared: PLEASE KEEP BREATHING. Then I started to cry, before she even had the chance to take a breath. She sent me out of the room, I was already torn to pieces, *It's eating away at my head*, she said. Which part of the story? I wanted to ask her. But she just slowly pushed me towards the door, and when we were by the door, she was in the room and I was out in the hallway. Is it all because of this story? I asked, trying to draw it out of her, but she shut the door in front of me and she was still inside the room, the misery was in me, and I was still standing outside in the hallway, no one ever wants the misery, and the door between us was separating her from me. I started banging on the door, which she then locked; at first I got aggressive, IF YOU DON'T LET ME IN I'LL KICK THIS DOOR DOWN, like a soldier, I thought, then I knocked more gently, I can't do this alone, I whispered at the white door. I didn't say it out of selfishness. That wasn't it. I was so helpless. Then the minutes went by, she stayed behind the closed door and I stopped knocking. And then, I beat my head against the door until I heard my wife crying. I stopped at once and rested my forehead on the door. I felt a thin trail of blood running from my temple down my face, I watched the thin line, stood there watching it, until my son called my name. I thought I'd heard my dead son's voice, I thought it had all been a bad dream, no disaster, no catastrophe, no misery that I'd have to get used to. Thank God, I cried and called for my wife, but then I realised that it was my son who was still alive.

The shame that came over me because I'd confused my dead child with my living one, I can't describe it. It's such a terrible feeling. I can't even bring myself to tell you about it. Don't write this part down. I turned right round to Diyar and wiped my forehead on my sleeve. My son had his rabbit in his arms, as usual. We went back into the living room.

Perhaps you're thinking you'll understand everything by the end of this story. There will be justice. But justice disappears when deaths happen. And perhaps you're thinking badly of me, but please don't think badly of my children.

When my son lay dying, I had no clue it was happening. When my son lay dying, my wife and I had already split up. She had a flat and I had a flat. I only saw my wife when I went to pick up the kids from hers. I was a bad father, my wife looked after our children. She did everything better than I did. I feel I can admit to that since my son's death, yes. When my son lay dying, I had gone to bed around half 10 as usual. I was at home. I had a small flat. Two bedrooms. A hallway. A bathroom. My wife had four bedrooms. A hallway. A bathroom. She also had the three children. I'm always talking about my sons, I hope my daughter will forgive me. My daughter, her name's Cansu, she's the eldest. Sometimes I forget she's still a child. She's grown up now but she's still my little girl. When my son died, Cansu wrapped herself in a blanket until she disappeared under the blanket. She cried so loudly that I was struck dumb. I stood in the hallway and watched my daughter. My wife's brother sat next to her on the sofa in the children's room. My Cansu was almost eighteen. She screamed, WHAT HAPPENED. It was beyond belief, what happened there. I screamed back from the hallway, THERE'S NOTHING TO

SEE HERE. Everyone who was standing around my daughter in that room, around the sofa my daughter was sitting on, wrapped in her blanket, they all turned to look at me. That was when they noticed me for the first time. And I said, There's nothing.

When my son died, I talked about him constantly. I'd walk out into the street and say to myself, This is where he stood. Then I'd point out the place I mentioned a few seconds ago and take a very close look at it. What was it I saw? I saw everything. There was a tree. A street and a house. A hotel. A petrol station. A bakery. I talked about my son so much that at some point no one wanted to listen to me anymore. It went on like that for months. Eventually, people would turn away from me whenever I mentioned his name. I began to curse myself. What else could I do? I went there every day. Where else could I go? I sat down on the bench near the street and started laughing until I couldn't stop. My belly was squeezing the air out of me and only then did I realise I wasn't laughing; I was screaming and hitting myself in the head. Could anyone still think straight in that situation? Eventually, I lost all interest in things. Who was going to make it okay? They come into the East from the West. What's in it for them? I threw stones into the street; I hit a car, then a man got out and he came and slapped me around. I stood up and fought him.

All I know is: PERSON B fired the shots because PERSON A ordered him to do it. PERSON A and PERSON B are policemen. Who do I hold to account? A policeman. Why do I have to kill a policeman? Because a policeman shot my son. It's stupid, I know. I promise you, believe me when I tell you: I'm not a cruel or crazy person.

Please don't get me wrong. I want nothing more than a normal life. A normal life is a safe life. The police hunt us down. They drag you to a station, you stay there 'til they tell you to Get lost. Soldiers hunt us down. They fire into the air, at you, and then they say, We've no other choice. What choices do we have? My only choice is to shoot someone. I want to defend myself. Who will I shoot? PERSON A, who gave the order, or PERSON B, who carried it out? I'll shoot both. Heaven, hell, justice. None of them exist. How does the violence here begin? With a gun? With a bullet? What does it achieve? Who's surprised when people fight back? Not me. I'm telling you: if there were any justice, all this would eventually end.

The funeral was held in November. There was snow on the ground. It wouldn't stop snowing, the snow almost came up to our knees. It was such a cold day that my van would only edge forward slowly. I got out and tried to push the car, but I kept sliding back. I pushed with all my might. Pushing, pushing. But my hands kept slipping because of the cold. I banged my head against the van – like I did with the door my wife lay behind, the van was white like the door in my wife's flat – then fell headfirst into the snow. Someone turned me over, I couldn't tell who it was at first, Let them come and get me, I said to my brother-in-law, who pulled me out of the snow.

Umut sighed and grabbed me by the scruff. He lay his head on my shoulder. Think of your other two children, he said quietly, and he pulled me to my feet so that I wasn't lying in the snow anymore, but standing in the snow. I thought I was going to freeze to death. My shoes were wet. I didn't freeze to death. My suit trousers were dirty. But I still wanted to fight back. My jacket was half hanging over my shoulder. The snow kept falling and I didn't know how to fight back. Please don't feel sorry for me, I deserve this. Because as my son lay dying, I was lying in bed.

More men came over to us. We pushed the van. Then suddenly, I don't know what got into me, I started beating my head, like I had on the door in my wife's flat, on the van. I kept doing it for such a long time, until finally three of them grabbed me and pulled me away.

EVERYTHING IN THIS COUNTRY, I yelled.
They said, Haydar, please.
I said, All of it.
Haydar, please, they said again.
Then Umut came over again and hugged me.
He whispered, I'm sorry, this is it.

Policemen and soldiers work together. They don't want justice. We already know that. I don't care who it was, Umut. I will find him. They live off the money they earn firing shots in our region. To protect the fatherland. Who does it satisfy? Not us. What are we supposed to do with it? They can have the fatherland. No really, I don't want it. And then I'll go. And I don't care if I'm shot dead. But it does frighten me. Because that's just how my son died. I looked into Umut's eyes for a long while and it was clear to me that he understands the weight I carry, he knows where the fire burns in this country; it burns here, it burns inside me and inside him too because he's my wife's brother. And my wife and I, we've fallen to pieces.

Please don't think we're bad parents, but our son was shot dead out in the street. My brother-in-law Umut came running that night. It was very late in the evening, I was already in bed, I can't get past that: I was in bed when my son lay dying, and I can't remember exactly but I think that I was already asleep, like the neighbours. And it wasn't the sound of shots that woke me; it was the knocking on the flat door. Umut came running that night and he hammered on the door like a madman. I woke with a start. I thought: *The soldiers are coming*. I thought: *It's the police*. In bed, I wondered what I'd done. What had I done? I promise you, I hadn't done anything. Our lives were always ordinary. I walked barefoot to the door without switching on the light. Ever so quietly, holding my breath, until Umut started screaming my name. It was only then that I realised it was him. I promise you: when I opened the door and saw the state he was in, I knew straight away that something had happened. Suddenly I was in a worse state than Umut. And I never came out of it. I'm still in it today.

Your son, he said.
Then he said, They hit your son.

I fell to the floor in front of Umut. That was all it took. In this country, hit means wounded. And in this country, wounded usually means dead. My flat was clean and tidy. I was in my pyjamas, lying in the hallway, thinking: *Who knew a world could end so easily?* My son had been hit by a bullet and I couldn't get it out of my head. I wasn't there but I imagined how it had happened. Why? I was foolish.

Umut and I drove straight to the hospital. My wife was already there, she said my name and I said hers, and then we were in each other's arms and my wife smelt like my son and I thought my chest was collapsing, no sound came out of me, Let their

159

fatherland collapse, I thought, but it wasn't collapsing and nor was my chest, and I wanted to punish myself for it, then I wanted to punish their fatherland, but I didn't know what a just punishment would be.

Our family and friends had gathered around us; they stood, like us, in the hospital corridor. I cried and cried and cried, in that moment I didn't care what else might happen. I couldn't tell who was there or who was standing next to me. It was one in the morning. The room where my son lay was not particularly big; we could only just fit us all in. My wife was the first to go inside and she was barely halfway in when she turned to face me. Her hands went to her face and held her mouth shut. For a few seconds my eyes clung to her hands and for a brief moment, everything was ok. I tried to convince myself: this is a state of peace. Nothing had happened. I said to myself, Nothing's happened. Then I said it to the others too. Then I heard my brother-in-law cry out, and at his cry, like a shot, I looked at my son, and I thought: I've become the way I am because of what I've been through.

My son had swollen up like a balloon. His stomach, his face, his arms. I couldn't tell where one tube started and the next ended. I DON'T RECOGNISE HIM, I said to our friends and family. No one wants to remember their child that way. He was so disfigured, it broke my heart. I took his hand, squeezed it, placed my hand over his hand, held it close. I took my wife's hand and lay it on top of my son's, then I lay my hand over it too. We looked at each other and we both knew he wouldn't survive. He was so badly battered. I don't want to talk about it. I can't. Please don't make me. I've had to struggle with the image in my head ever since that day. In my head, it's not my son I see; I see a young man on the street, shot down by some policeman. He was bloated by the bullets. He died at the hospital three hours later.

If you haven't been through anything like this before, I'm glad for you. No one should have to go through anything like it. I'm afraid of the picture I can't hold back. Seriously, it's another thing that stops me sleeping. I failed as a father. I failed to protect my son.

My son didn't pass at home. He never opened his eyes again, never saw us again, never spoke to us again. He didn't listen to us. We told him, Please don't die. Let us die for you. We're your parents. Let us die. My clever, handsome Devin, he was sixteen years old. He died in hospital, while in the hallway and in that hospital room his family and friends waited for something other than death. My son Devin died as my wife and I clung to his hand. I whispered, before it was over, into my son's ear, I will find them. My wife cried, HOW IS ANYONE MEANT TO GET USED TO THIS, as my son stopped breathing.

We didn't tell Diyar that we were going to his brother's funeral. Diyar thought, even weeks later, that his brother had been taken to another country on an aeroplane. Diyar thought his brother was going to get the medical care he needed in another country. We didn't say that his brother had been shot; we said his brother had a sickness in his head. We went to Devin's funeral but we told Diyar we were collecting money for the tests his brother needed. Diyar asked what the sickness in his brother's head looked like. I showed him a map and on the map I pointed to this country. Then I held his hand tight and showed him all the people who had come along. Diyar was glad and thought they were all there to help his brother. My Diyar is not a stupid child, my Diyar is just a child.

The funeral was held in secret in a rented hall. Large gatherings were forbidden and in the end we registered the funeral as a wedding. If the police had got wind of the funeral, they would have crashed the funeral. Then I would have lost it completely. But disguising a funeral as a wedding is shameful enough as it is. I curse it all. The hall had lots of rooms. We put the children in one room. In one room were the toilets. There was a corridor, where we hung a big picture of Devin. The women carried the coffin in on their shoulders. We threw flowers onto it while Diyar played in the room where we had put all the children. He had brought his rabbit in a shoebox. That morning, my wife had put on light-coloured trousers and a white shirt. Diyar didn't ask me or his mother why we were dressed differently to normal. I stood with carnations in my arms and I looked at the big picture of Devin hanging on the wall with carnations in my arms. I don't want to know how much Diyar has understood. I hope he hasn't picked up on anything. That's naïve of me, I know, but I couldn't bring myself to tell him the truth. Whatever for? It was the afternoon and we were burying our son.

Then my wife and I and my two children went to my wife's flat. Cansu was in her room and had shut the door behind her. My wife went back into the bedroom she'd come out of before we went to the funeral, and she lay back down on the bed, on the side she always sleeps on. Diyar and I went into the living room; I switched on the TV, sat down on the sofa and wondered if my child would still be alive in a different country without all the police and soldiers there are in this country.

A few days after the funeral, soldiers came to my wife's flat. They said, You buried a terrorist. They smashed the glass cabinets in the living room, took swings at the pictures of my children hanging in the hall until the pictures fell to the floor. They walked over my children's faces with their boots, then dragged my two children from their beds. Cansu was quiet and Diyar was only worried about his rabbit. The last thing they did was pull my wife out of the bedroom; her hands and feet kicked out as she struggled. They lined us up in the living room. It wasn't until they smashed the TV to pieces that I realised what they were doing. All they said was, Ten minutes. We put on our jackets, that was all we could manage, the ten minutes passed like ten seconds. You know, there's nothing you can do when there's an armed unit standing in front of you, in front of your children; their guns are as long as my arm. I put my children in the back of the car. My wife sat in the passenger seat. I got into the car last. Through the mirror, my wife and I watched the soldiers smashing up our home. They broke all the windows from the outside. Inside, they threw out the furniture. They sprayed a red X on the front door before heading back inside. I turned the key in the ignition – I wanted to spare us this moment, it was more than enough already, everything that had happened – but my wife placed her hand on mine and said, Wait. The curtains were set alight. Then they burned. What more was there to see?

Don't do this to yourself, I said to my wife.
She replied, It reeks.

I know they get their orders from above. I know that someone commands them to comb the area until they find what they're meant to be looking for, but I still wonder how they sleep at night. Maybe they do love the fatherland. But it can't really count for that much. Can it? It's all a bit off. They can come and drive us out of our homes and villages and cities, kill our children first and then kill us, out of love for their fatherland or the belief that they love their fatherland, because they're doing something good for the fatherland they love, but I can't love it. The question that seems most pressing to me is: how do they sleep at night? I think they go to bed in their uniforms. So that if something happens at night, at the barracks or on the battle field, they can be ready to go, straight away. I think that because they get their orders from above, they think they're absolved of the harm they cause. But I'm telling you, they aren't.

I took my family to the home of my wife's eldest brother. I couldn't think of anywhere better. My children hugged me before they got out of the car. My wife sat next to me a while longer.

Where are you going to go? She asked me.
I'm going to look for them until I find them.
Don't end up like them, she said.

Then she got out. I watched her walk up to her brother's house. When she reached the front door, she turned back to look at me again. We were married for twenty years, and that moment, outside a door again, was the last time we saw each other. Back then, I didn't know it would be the last. I thought I was going to look for what I had to find, like the soldiers, then go back to my family. But what exactly was I looking for? It was only when I drove away that I realised my wife had already had an inkling of what it meant, her standing in front of the door and me being in the car, for how the story would turn out. Before she got out of the car, she handed me the ring she wore on her left index finger. It was a gold ring her mother had given her when she was the same age Cansu is now. I'd always known how much the ring meant to her, and giving me the ring was her way of saving a scrap of grace and hope for us in this story.

The night before the funeral, while my children were asleep but the TV was still on, I saw Umut. He gave me a photo. In the photo was a man. The man in the photo was probably my age, or maybe younger or older than me. His clothes were plain. He wasn't wearing a uniform. He was smiling at the camera. This is him, Umut said. I believed him without asking how he knew. He said he'd make sure that the person found me so that I could shoot the person. He didn't say how he hoped to make it happen. But Umut didn't just say that sort of thing for nothing. I learned from Umut that the man was a policeman. Umut talks about policemen all day long. But you know, like Umut, I've never trusted the police in this country. I've always said that. We'll keep talking about it until you understand where we're coming from. We come into this world alone and we'll leave it alone too, that's a given. But if we don't do anything to fight police violence, things will never get better here.

On the back of the picture, Umut wrote:

You should go to Germany
And never come back
There's nothing here
That they don't have there
There's nothing here but sleeping dogs

Then we hugged and I knew that a man with a gun will shoot

even if he's asleep. What else is left? How am I supposed to sleep at night? Soldiers sleep in their uniforms, like there's nothing in their days that keeps them awake. Their duty is to defend their territory. My duty is to protect my children and keep them safe from harm.

Then I sat in the car and I didn't know where to start looking for the man in the photograph. I had a picture but little else to go on. I didn't even ask when the picture was taken. You know, I was in the car with the radio on, but I was focussing on the mirror, and I saw a police car that had been behind me for much too long. The song on the radio was still playing when they cut me off to make me stop the car. They pulled up beside me. They opened my car door and one of them grabbed me by my jacket collar, like Umut had when he'd pulled me out of the snow on the day of the funeral; inside the car I was wearing a black leather jacket and my head knocked against the windscreen with the same force I'd hit the closed bedroom door with when my wife didn't want to come out of her room. Where are you off to? they asked. Thank God I was on my own. They pushed me to the ground, hands on my back, one of them kicked me in the ribs. They took me to the police station and shoved me in a cell. The cell was smaller than my car. I don't know how many days I spent sitting there. Sometimes they'd come in and beat me, then they'd leave. Then one night they grabbed me again, beat me and left me lying out in the street.

I'm here now and it doesn't matter how I got here. There are two of us living in this flat. We don't talk much. But that's okay. At night, when Murat sleeps and I sit at the window keeping watch, he dreams. And when Murat dreams, he has nightmares; then he tells me, My mother's in the cupboard. I'm a brute. Some nights I run into his room to wake him up. Then he goes quiet. I wake him up and he says, I dreamt about how things were before. I could already tell that when I stood in the doorway watching him pulling at the air in his sleep as if he was trying to dig himself out of the ground. Then I went back to my chair. I don't dream about how things were before. Murat has never spoken openly with me about the time before – before we ended up here – but I don't think that's a bad thing. I see what's bothering him. It bothers me too. But we both know, and we don't have to talk about it.

We lived together for three years. Then policemen came and took him away. The room I sit in can only be seen from the hallway if you stand at the right angle to the door. Murat didn't tell them that I was in the flat. I heard them beating him and I kept looking out of the window. It lasted a few minutes. I know, you must be wondering why I did nothing to help him. It was terrible, believe me. But I had a gun in my hand. When police see guns in our hands, they panic. If they had seen the gun, they would have shot me and then Murat. Murat said, I'm right here – I understood at once that he was talking to me.

The police burst out laughing and said,
We've got you.
In a normal voice, Murat said, My mother.
Do you want your mummy you little pussy, is that what you want? they mocked.

I heard the front door open. There was no sound of Murat anymore, then the door shut. Behind the closed door I kept sitting there motionless in my chair. From where I was sitting,

I watched them put Murat in the police car. From down there, he looked up at me. Then they drove away.

I took the plastic zip-up laundry bag out of the cupboard. I stood in Murat's room with the laundry bag in my hand and looked at his bed. He had still been there that morning. Then I ran out the flat. Down the steps. Taking good care. Down the steps. And then I was outside. I probably ran for over an hour. I reached an open space. I crossed into a field next to the road. There were almost 700 kilometres between us and our hometown. I dug a hole, until the hole was big enough. Then I put the plastic zip-up laundry bag inside and covered the hole over. But the real question is: what sort of person could accept all this? And I'm telling you, we don't accept it. Then I ran back.

When I got back to the flat, I sat at the table and tried to draw the route to the grave. I thought someone from Murat's family might come and look for him, then they'd find the drawing and know that Murat's mother was okay. I put the drawing in Murat's cupboard, behind the chair with all the clothes on it, where his mother had been hiding the whole time.

That was the last thing I did. Now I can hear them in the stairwell. They're calling for me. I don't know who sent them. They're getting closer and I'm still sitting on the chair, looking out. I was watching them from the window. The street couldn't swallow up their noise. Soon they'll break the door down. I think of Devin first of all. In the stairwell, they shout:

ANYONE WHO BURIES A TERRORIST IS A TERRORIST.

I hope my son can forgive me for this life. Write this down: justice won't make a broken life any better if it comes too late.

02:55

EPISODE EIGHT: METİN

> Metin lives on the second floor. Metin likes red
> carnations. Metin is deaf in his right ear. Metin counts
> the days backwards. Metin doesn't want to stay here.

I went through the worst torture in prison. You could never
be sure when it was going to happen. Sometimes they'd come
at four in the afternoon. Sometimes at midday. Sometimes in
the middle of the night or at five in the morning. You didn't
know when they might turn up. But you knew for certain
that they were going to come. They would burst into our cells
and beat us. They'd burst into our cells, pull us out and beat
us. Or they'd burst into our cells, drag us out of our cells one
after the other with kicks and punches, and gather us out in
the courtyard.

They ordered us to *STRIP* until we were naked.

They kept beating us as we undressed. If you took longer to
undress, you'd get more of a beating than the others. And if
one of us was too slow, the others would be beaten, too. We
stood naked in the concrete yard and they sprayed us with
ice cold water. They'd do this on a whim, sometimes every
day. The prison boss, a big, furious man, stepped forward and
said, ON YOUR BACKS. The water seeped across the floor.
This was winter, spring, summer, autumn. We lined up in the
concrete courtyard and we were freezing. We were forced to
keep our legs fifteen centimetres off the ground and stay like
that until the prison boss had gone down the line and – one

prisoner after another, what with all the time he had, he had nothing else to do, after all, but fill his time in the prison with beatings – beat our feet bloody with a piece of wood.

Winter, spring, summer, autumn. We continued to freeze on the ground. He would walk from one prisoner to the next, almost gleeful. The other men – the guards, guards wear uniforms too – watched their boss. They forced us to sing their military songs while he beat us. They were terrible songs. It makes you wonder what's worse about prison: the songs or the beatings? My eardrum burst. At first I thought it was the songs that did it. But it was the beatings that left me deaf in my right ear. These days, if I go somewhere and there's music on the radio, I can hardly bear it. I either have to leave the room or switch the radio off, but usually I switch the radio off and leave the room all the same.

I'm keen to put it behind me. I'll only relay the essentials. And if that's not enough, there's nothing I can do to change it. My name is Metin. It's not my real name, but it's what they call me here. I spent four years in prison. My head was shaved. When I left prison and went back to my family, they didn't recognise me. They were counting the days until I could be back with them. I was counting the days backwards: days that had passed since my incarceration. I had no visitors during my time in prison. If my family came to visit, I'd be pulled out of the cell and put in a waiting room. My family didn't come. The guards would say, Visiting hours are over. It's only with hindsight that I've come to realise they were doing it to bully me, sticking me in the waiting room without telling my family. When my family came to visit, they were also put in a waiting room. They'd have to stay there for hours until the guards came and told them, Visiting hours are over. The letters I wrote to my family never reached them.

Instead, a guard would come into my cell once a week – I could set the time by his visit. He would kick me in the stomach. He'd turn me on my back. One booted foot would land on my ribcage. He would slam his full weight down on me; I'd cough and worry that I'd be sent to the concrete courtyard again, naked in the water, four walls, everything around me grey. The guard pulled one of the letters I'd written to my family out of his jacket and held it in front of my nose. Yes, I knew the story about the rat too, it made me sick. It made everyone sick. You know, life's short, but in prison, dying just takes longer. I thought: *They're not going to break me* – but what did I know. The guard stuck a finger in my mouth. It came as quite a surprise to me. He pressed at least three of his fingers against my teeth, my front teeth both top and bottom. At some point we both, by that I mean the guard and I, heard a crack. My incisors gave way under the force of his fingers, and more than two of his fingers went through the gaps in my teeth into the back of my throat. I winced, and when I did so he managed to open my mouth. He screwed up the letter until the letter fit inside my mouth. *It says here we shaved your head?* I got a beating for that. *You did it yourself.* He kept beating me. *Filthy son of a bitch.* I spent my twenty-second, twenty-third, twenty-fourth and twenty-fifth birthdays in prison.

Prison is a dirty hole. The guards in there have their moral code and we prisoners have our own. Our code helps combat their violence and the guards' moral code justifies their violence towards us. That's where we differ from each other. That's how it is in prison: in the guards' eyes, we're animals. We're behind bars and they're on the other side, standing outside our cells with clubs. We're their very own beating zoo. You're thinking: *They're not animals,* but they say, We'll string you up like dogs. Dogs are worth nothing in this country and now they've got us kennelled. In prison, guards forget that they're human beings and that their prisoners are human beings too.

For its inmates, prison is like an artificial coma. You're awake but ripped away from life. Time stands still somehow. You can't really talk or think. Four years in, it stopped. One day guards came storming into my cell, I thought I was about to be beaten again but they grabbed me under my arms and dragged me out. You've been released for now, they said. Go on, fuck off. I was sad to have to leave my friends behind.

I've been out of prison for nine years. This is where I live now. I sit here every day, on a plastic chair outside the door to the tower block, watching what happens on the street. Policemen come sometimes. One kicks my chair and yells:

DON'T YOU HAVE A HOME TO GO TO, DONKEY BRAIN? WHAT'S THE POINT OF SITTING AROUND OUTSIDE THE DOOR ALL DAY?

I don't get into a discussion. I just lie there on the ground and stay there until they're done talking. When they move on, I get up and sit back down on the chair. That's a normal day for me.

When I left prison and came home, I didn't recognise my family. I felt like one of those soldiers who come home from the army having lost something on the battlefield or on the border. Like me, they no longer recognise things and have become unrecognisable too. I got off the bus and walked past my family. There were people standing everywhere, waiting for someone. To my eyes, one head just gave way to the next head. I couldn't see people anymore, only potential attackers. I thought there were bound to be guards among them, just waiting for the right moment to step forward and beat me again. At first, I thought that that was how the torture would continue; that they had released me for fun just so they could arrest me again once I was off the bus. It might sound strange to you, but anything is possible in this country. My cousin ran up behind me and put a hand on my shoulder. He was probably trying to get my attention – I was weaving left to right like a madman, after all – but it sent me straight back to my cell and I started hitting him. His wife and my mother grabbed me and held me back until I had calmed down.

It's only us, he said.
It's hard, I replied.

In the first weeks, I couldn't really talk to them properly. Around every corner I expected to see a guard. Sometimes I would burst out screaming. It came out of nowhere. I'd see or hear something that reminded me of prison, then something in my head would blow. My mother looked at me with horror in her eyes and stood rooted to the spot. Everything got my hackles up, Why is everything different? I asked several times a day.

You know, I'm one of those people who bottles everything up. Sometimes it helps, but sometimes it doesn't. I couldn't talk about the prison itself. When my family tried to coax it out of me, I couldn't find an answer. I sat in front of them, my hands folded over one another, and I didn't know what to say to them. Eventually, they stopped asking. I felt better then. Even if I had talked about it, who would I be doing it for? What would it change for my family if they found out what it was like in there? I don't think talking about it would achieve anything. Everything runs on orders there. When I talk about orders, it's almost like I'm giving orders myself. Please don't get me wrong; there's a difference between acceptance and reality. I can accept the reality, and that's the time I spent inside, but I can't accept the situation this country forces us into.

My family picked me up from the bus station. Then we walked to the carpark. We got into the car. My cousin at the front, my mother next to him. I sat behind the driver's seat, and my cousin's wife sat next to me. It was only once I got in the car that I started to feel safer. It was so peculiar. As if my body had shrunk. The danger (guards) comes from outside (not inside the cells). I wasn't safe until I was inside the car (like in the cells). Yes, that was it. But actually, when I think back now, I realise it wasn't my body that shrank, it was the country.

We had been driving for over two hours when I realised that something wasn't right. I don't know why it only occurred to me then. WHERE'S BARAN? I yelled out of nowhere. I took my jacket off because I couldn't smell anything and I thought it was because I'd started sweating. And then I said, COME ON OUT, BARAN. I put my arm around my cousin's neck from behind. What possessed me in that moment? I didn't know. I still don't know what came over me. My conscience was probably tormenting me because my friends were still sitting in a cell and I wasn't. Part of me had stayed inside. I sat in a moving car. My arm shot around my cousin's neck; I think

I was squeezing the air out of him. Everything felt briefly suspended and I think I had taken my cousin for a guard who had Baran in his grip. STOP THE CAR, STOP THE CAR, said my mother. STOP IT, said Fidan, my cousin's wife. My cousin sped into the opposite lane but then came to a stop on the side of the road. We wrote you a letter, my mother said through her tears. They thought I already knew. How's that supposed to work? But it wasn't until I was in the moving car that I noticed Baran wasn't there to pick me up.

Where does it hurt most? my cousin asked.
Everywhere, I said.

My mother took an envelope out of the lining of her jacket. The letter my family had written to me in prison, which hadn't reached me in prison but was sent back to them, went like this:

It's early morning as we write to you. We think of you every day. Your mother wonders: Is my son getting enough to eat, is my son sleeping in a bed, on the floor or on a table, are they tormenting him? Metin, I choose to imagine that they're not tormenting you. Every day we wait. But nothing comes. What have they done to you? And what can we do to stop them?

We buried your cousin yesterday. We found him lifeless on the side of the road a few days ago. We can't tell you any more than that. But we won't tell you what state we found him in. Every home and every picture is a reminder of how things used to be – and that's good too, it keeps us from forgetting what happened. What happened? We know what happened.

We are sending you a picture of your cousin. For you to remember

the times when we were all together. When you think of him, re-
member him only as he is in this picture.

I won't show you the picture of Baran. It holds too many sad
and difficult feelings for me. I can't talk about them. I can
show you other pictures instead, so that I don't have to think
of the picture of Baran. For me, the worst thing was that I was
in prison, oblivious. I didn't know what had happened. No.
I lay in my cell while my cousin lay on the side of the road.
That is something I can never change. My life consists of two
episodes: one episode is the length of my life before prison; the
other episode is my life afterwards.

I had to read the letter three times until I'd really understood it
all. Then I opened the car door and ran away. Out of my cell.
Out of my cell. Yes, that's what I thought. My cousin ran after
me. I didn't know where we were or where I was running to. I
just ran. Eventually, he caught up with me. It wasn't difficult; I
came out of prison sick and haggard. My cousin ran up to me
at full speed and slammed into me with his arms around my
chest, then we fell to the ground. On the ground, I cried because I realised in his embrace that I wasn't in prison anymore.

Then he let go of me, helped me up and brushed the dirt
off my jacket. We got back into the car. I sat back down behind my cousin, on the backseat next to his wife. My cousin
watched me in the rearview mirror the whole time. My mother
wasn't sitting in her seat normally. What I mean is, she wasn't
looking forwards; she turned towards me and watched me the
whole journey. I can still recognise you if I look very closely,
she said, lighting a cigarette.

Was it soldiers? I asked my cousin.

He nodded.

I don't think soldiers like being stationed in our region. Most of them have never been here before. And it's usually their first time away from their families. Everyone finds that hard. I understand. One of them said, We don't trust you. Another said, My mother didn't want me to end up here. In the past, I would have said, We don't want you here either. They're homesick the first time they come here. They learn what they're taught and what other soldiers learned before them. A commanding officer gets a map of the country, splits the land into two parts: West and East. The North is part of the West and the South is part of the East. And he points and says, This is where they're hiding. Soldiers learn to shoot to find terrorists. They protect their comrades, when necessary, and also when they get into fights with each other. In the mornings they go up into the mountains and in the evenings they come back down to their barracks. Then they say, No one wants to stay up there. The atmosphere is one of camaraderie, it's probably the only way to endure their military service. Camaraderie changed a lot of things between inmates in prison too. It was the only way I made it through. Over time, my fellow inmates became my friends. Without them, I wouldn't have had the will to keep living. I'm very grateful for that, even though we went through something terrible. Take solitary confinement, for instance: no one can endure that. And looking back, you can't blame them. You sleep on your own. You sit there on your own. You eat on your own. And when you go into the courtyard to exercise, you do that on your own too. It's torture. Things are depressing enough in there, but then you're all alone too. No one can take it. Lots of men go mad. I would definitely have gone mad. I wouldn't have been able to take it. I can say that quite honestly.

My family told me that the fighting broke out at night. I listened closely as they talked. The next morning they knew there would be dead bodies. The soldiers gathered up the bodies and carried them to the playing field, where they were laid out next to one another. They were all civilians. All people we knew. The locals started to protest. The soldiers were pelted with stones. The people who threw the stones were arrested. Baran wasn't among the dead bodies on the ground at the playing field. Baran wasn't found until a few days later, off the side of the street. I lay red carnations on Baran's grave. I didn't comment on his death. It really surprised my family. In the past, I would have been more forceful. They were confusing the person I've become with the person I used to be. If you don't talk and keep things to yourself, you can't get beaten. But don't get me wrong; the good thing is, even if I don't talk about everything, that doesn't mean it has passed me by. It's not like I fell silent; I just stopped expressing certain things. By that I mean: there were things I kept inside. Every day, I lay a red carnation on Baran's grave. My condition worsened thanks to the ongoing military presence in our city. I was released from prison but I found myself in a different prison instead.

In prison, they would tell us: This is not a prison, it's an army barracks. Our job is to make you the same as us.

In the city, they would say: Anyone who resists is acting against the state and will be immediately arrested.

If you ask me, I'd say that's the same sentence twice, just

worded differently. Anti-terror units did the rounds in the city, and in prisons it was the guards. I didn't even feel safe in our flat. I couldn't leave the house on my own anymore. As soon as I saw uniformed men, I'd start to turn back. My cousin tried to explain the situation, but the units grew suspicious. What's up with him? they'd say. My cousin would shrug dully, Oh, he's just mad, he'd lie.

Are you a nutjob? they'd ask me.
Yes, I'd shout.

The fighting in our city found its way to me and grew more and more violent. At night I'd go to bed in my clothes; it was really the only way to calm myself down. I was scared that soldiers, policemen, guards could burst into our flats at any moment. At night I slept with the window open. That way, if they crept into the house by the door I'd be ready, dressed and could escape through the window of the flat, which would become a cell as soon as they came in. But things got much worse. Curfews tightened and attacks went on for longer. Shops were looted. Animals were shot. There were constant arrests. The units said, They were terrorists. But we knew it wasn't true. They said, Terror lives in the East. But by that, they actually meant all of us. The fighting was worse at night than it was in the mornings. Everyone attacked at night. My cousin and his wife had a kiosk. One day, an anti-terror unit came into their shop and accused my cousin, and then his wife, of being terrorists. The whole neighbourhood saw. We protested briefly but they ransacked the kiosk, though they didn't beat my cousin or his wife. Then they pilfered fruit, vegetables and drinks. On the street, the boss said, If you shop at a terrorist's shop, you're a terrorist too. And I'll shoot every terrorist dead myself. My cousin had to shut his shop. But there was no let-up. As soon as more than six people were seen together, soldiers would arrive and accuse all of them. They would say, We know what you're up to. Then they'd beat them with cudgels.

By that time we could only communicate with looks. Like in prison. I think that was also why my condition still hadn't improved. Language was lacking in the outside world too. I bottled everything up but it weighed heavily on me.

The city was unrecognisable. It smelt like gunpowder all day long. At night the fields burned and in the daytime children died, accidentally stepping on soldiers' mines as they played.

The car was the only place you'd still feel safe. By that I mean, in a moving car, driving along the road at least 60 mph. It was only at that speed, with the windows open, that we felt safe to talk. Yet there were never more than two people in a car at one time. Anything else, so more than two people, might have looked suspicious if we were stopped. I sat in the driver's seat as my cousin explained that he had to leave town. In the moving car, I thought: *We've changed.*

They came in the night, smashed the flat to pieces. One soldier said, Bring me that son of a bitch! They didn't find my cousin. He was already gone. They trashed the entire flat until everything was broken. Are you crazy? I asked. You're a bold one, aren't you, you prick. He took his gun and hit me in the nose; it started bleeding. Then they left. Before I thought of Baran, I thought of his brother, my cousin. May God help him. Thirty-three people were arrested and taken to the playing field again, where they were lined up together in a row.

The commanding officer said, *I don't see any way out if you keep on like this. What do we do with vermin like you?* He fired into the air five times.

My cousin's wife was suddenly standing next to me. I looked at her for a long time to try to work out if it was bad news. The good news was they hadn't caught my cousin, but the bad news was it was now my turn, as punishment for not catching him. I handled this better than I'd expected. I went back home; I didn't run. I lay a red carnation on Baran's grave and I gave a red carnation to my mother and to my cousin's wife. We've learned to handle the truth, but the soldiers can't handle the fact that we tell the truth.

Now I'm here and what else is there to say? There are nice people living here, people from my neck of the woods. Sometimes I act like I'm back home. Everyone sits around all day here. They ask a question and no one answers, so they answer their questions themselves.

Nurten asks, When are my sons coming home?

Everyone is silent.

She says, All we can do is hope they'll be back soon.

Nurten doesn't know it, but two of her three sons never even made it to prison. One was kidnapped in a car, blindfolded. The other was shot next to the car in cold blood. I'm deliberately using that phrase, in cold blood, because it was an execution in cold blood. There's no other fitting way to describe an execution. If you kill people in front of other people, it can only be in cold blood. They threw the body in a well. Then they concreted over the well. It wasn't soldiers that did it, no. It was spies, because they behave like soldiers too. They come and shoot you and make you disappear under concrete. I heard this from Nurten's son Erdem; he was standing there in handcuffs while one of the brothers sat in the car blindfolded and heard the shot that killed the other brother who wasn't blindfolded. Erdem and I shared a cell for over a year. I find it hard to think about it. I had to leave Erdem behind in the cell.

Every day, I buy five carnations. One carnation for Baran, another for my cousin, one for my mother, for Fidan, and the last is always for Erdem. When you're in prison, knowing that there's someone outside thinking of you does wonders.

Erdem said, My mother can never find out.
I replied, I don't talk as much as I used to.

I know that Nurten goes into her sons' room every day. I'm there sometimes. She sits on a chair. Then she takes some piece of clothing out of the cupboard and smells the clothing.

Then Nurten goes into the kitchen and gives me two bags full of bread. She bakes bread every day. I don't know who she does it for. You're like Erdem, she said to me once, you keep everything bottled up.

I don't know if people know what's going on here. I don't know if they only know a little or if they know everything. I put one of the bags of bread outside the two girls' hiding place. They're not from around here either and they only leave their hideout at night. Their hiding place is in the hallway. In the hallway there's a false floor in the ceiling. They lie there all day until it gets dark.

They say, They want to lock us up.
I say, We're far away now.

My prison was a concrete yard. Their prison is in the hallway above the ceiling. I'm almost thirty-five now. Hêlîn and Sara haven't been to prison but they kill time as if they were. You probably can't imagine that; I don't want to picture it myself either. It's almost like they're obeying some invisible command. They sleep during the day. On their backs or on their bellies. At night they get up, eat something, then go back to sleep. That's their work. They lie there, then they get up, then they lie down again. The prison is 500 kilometres from here, but when I watch how they get up and creep out of their hiding place at night, I think: I've got a piece of prison inside me. My hands are bound; I'd love to tell them, We're not lost. The future will be better.

Sometimes they come out during the day. But only when it's almost dark. Then they sit with Nurten, or in silence with Hasso. They lie flat on the ground when they do it, like they do in their hiding place, so that no one can see their heads. Some evenings, Hêlîn begins to cry without anyone hearing her. Sara sits next to her and runs the inside of her hand over Hêlîn's face and blots her tears away. I usually sit across from them and think about Erdem. There are regular raids here. I'm sure I've forgotten something important that's happened and haven't really managed to share everything. But soldiers count down the days on their fingers. And along with the days, they count the people they deem to be terrorists and who they've killed. Then they say, Forty-seven dead terrorists are forty-seven fewer threats to our country. They take aim and we fall down because their bullets strike civilians on purpose. Their mission is over for now. Our misery will be over when they come into our homes. They're in Nurten's flat now.

They say, Come out!
We say, We're not armed
and put our arms up.

First Nurten, then me. Hasso looks at the floor. They carry Hasso away and Nurten runs after them. I stand around, useless, unmoving, and the soldiers who are still in the room close in on me. They put their hands on their guns. What happened to you, you moron? says their boss and slaps me round the face. I creep inside myself. It's polite to answer when I ask you a question, he says and slaps me again. I wish death on all guards. Soldiers too. Honestly, it's no less than they deserve. Don't get me wrong – I'm actually opposed to violence; I want to sit in the grass and watch bugs, not fear for my life, but at some point it's got to stop. The army's bombs explode close to us. It's deliberate. They make you go strange in the head. Winter, spring, summer, autumn. When you're not right in the head, you walk slower. North and West. East and South. And the soldiers eat the fruit and vegetables from my cousin's kiosk.

When they catch their so-called terrorists, meaning us, they put us in a small empty room. In this small empty room, they hang their flag on the wall. They stand us in front of the flag and take a picture. Then they say:

YOU WANTED TO SPLIT THIS COUNTRY IN TWO

– BUT NOW WE'VE GOT A PICTURE OF YOU WITH OUR FLAG. THIS PHOTO IS PROOF THAT YOU CAN'T SPLIT OUR COUNTRY IN TWO.

Hêlîn and Sara are in their hiding place. I'm the only one who knows they're there. I had to leave Erdem behind in prison. He's probably lying on the floor because there are no beds in the cells. Hêlîn and Sara are lying above me. If the danger had passed, I would go back to my family and lay a red carnation on Baran's grave. Then I'd get into a car. The windows would be open and I'd drive straight on for as long as I could. You know, it's exile, what's happening here. And in this exile, soldiers and guards think their actions are justified. Who's right? A strong army is made of men who accept violence. And the army in this country only adds to the damage, but the greater the damage, the smaller the country becomes.

He's mentally backward the boss explains.
Shall we throw a hand grenade at you to wake you up a bit?
Then he shows me his hand grenade.

I left my life behind in prison. I forget nothing; I'd like to tell him that, but in truth, I just don't talk about how much I know.

15:48

EPISODE NINE: DEVRİM

Devrim doesn't live in the tower block. Devrim knows
what a G3 looks like. Devrim talks to his aunt on the
telephone. Devrim packs his rucksack and gets on the bus.

I wear a chain around my neck. It's a silver chain. The chain
has a heart-shaped locket. Inside the heart-shaped locket is
a picture. In the picture are two children. One of the children is my brother and the other child is me. We're sitting in
the grass outside our house with our arms around each other.
We're both wearing jeans. My brother is wearing a blue jumper.
Mine is grey. Our father took the picture of my brother and
me. Our mother is standing behind us. She's wearing jeans,
too, and a white blouse.

Soldiers tied my grandfather to a tree. They used thin ropes,
beige ones. You can do damage with ropes. My father watched
as they did it, and my grandfather knew my father was watching. My father ran away after my grandfather screamed at him
to run away. His son, my father, turned on the spot; he was
wearing a light grey t-shirt and brown corduroy trousers, and
he ran in the opposite direction. Over the road, up a slope.
Behind him were mountains, rocks. In front of him, too. In
front of the mountains were his father and the soldiers. You
can do damage with ropes. Soldiers know this. My father was
wearing cheap plastic shoes in dark brown, the kind that stink
when you stand in the sun for too long. He hid behind a rock
and watched the soldiers surround his father. One of them
grabbed him by the shoulders and shoved him in front of a

tree. The tree had a thick trunk and green leaves. His father, my grandfather, couldn't defend himself. One of them, probably the group's commanding officer, pushed my grandfather so that his back was flat against the tree. Then they tied him to it. You can do damage with ropes. My grandfather was fifty-five years old.

They tied rope number one around his shoulders, looped it around the tree trunk once and knotted it tight in front of his chest. The next rope went around his hips. They pulled it taut. They looped it around the tree and my grandfather many times. Pull, taut and tie. His hands were already tied behind his back. Last of all, they tied one around his legs, level with his thighs. And taut, taut. You can do damage with ropes. My father told me, Five soldiers stood around my father in a semi-circle. The other soldiers – there were five or six more men who weren't standing in the semi-circle – were sitting on the ground. Either on rocks or in the grass. The grass was green and lush. They set down their guns next to them; some even took their boots off, then their socks, shoving them into their boots, and put their bare feet in the grass. It was a little clearing that people didn't pass by often. It was up in the mountains.

A few trees, mountains, rocks, stones and, between them, the anti-terror units sent from the city to storm the mountains, ambushing them with the command, TAKE AIM, FIRE. A soldier says, THERE'S A TERRORIST LYING IN WAIT BEHIND THAT ROCK – if a mountain appears behind the rock. Then they fire at the rock. When no one emerges from behind the rock or is laid low by their bullets, they say, THEY'RE TRYING TO LURE US INTO A TRAP. They circle the rock. When there's really no one behind it, they stand before the mountain. On the far side of the mountain there's a cave, so they say THE AMBUSH IS IN THE CAVE. Any soldier who is mad enough – and up in the mountains madness means men who feel like heroes in their uniforms, men who leave everything behind for their fatherland – storms the cave and screams, NO ONE CAN SPLIT OUR COUNTRY IN TWO, NOT EVEN TERRORISTS. They split my grandfather into three and bound him to a tree with ropes. It was May. May is the most beautiful time of year up there in the mountains. Did you know that? No? Well, now you do.

The soldiers who weren't standing in a circle around my grandfather were smoking cigarettes on the rocks, on the ground, or pulling up grass. The soldiers sitting in the grass with their guns next to them, pulling up grass or smoking, didn't look at my grandfather once. In hindsight, I think they didn't look because they performed the tasks they were commanded to do like a job. You don't have to look every time. That's how you adjust. People who adjust also adjust to their comrades and keep searching for terrorists behind rocks up in the mountains. But there's a worry at the heart of a soldier's life. For them the worry begins with us, but it came here with them. For soldiers, their concern for the fatherland begins with traitors to the fatherland. And in their eyes, every traitor to the fatherland has forfeited a place in this country. There was no charge. My grandfather wasn't on any wanted list, no one was looking for him.

My father stared at the hands of a soldier pulling up grass. Later on he told me, I didn't know what I was doing. His eyes remained fixed on the hands. And by the time he heard the shots, it was too late. They killed my grandfather, his father,

195

with two bullets. The soldiers on the ground, on the rock, smoked their cigarettes down to the butt. The one who'd been pulling up the grass kept pulling. It was a normal day in May for them. And it was a day in May. For my father, it was a day in May when hands reminded him of grass and grass of hands. He said, It stalks us across the whole country. Soldiers had nothing to lose back then. And when they had to go back into the mountains, they went with their comrades. They talked, fired and slept, and when they came down from the mountains into the city, they'd say, It's cold up there when it rains. That meant the soldiers would be on the road again eventually. My father pressed his body to the ground behind the rock. Everyone knew that if soldiers turned up, there'd be bodies. But when it happens to you, it all becomes harder to believe. When their military service is over, soldiers are discharged and allowed to go home, but our dead stay in the ground.

He said, They say, Terrorists hide behind rocks.

But I'm telling you: if they had realised that my grandfather wasn't alone and my father was hiding, they'd have said, THERE'S YOUR PROOF and they'd have fired at him from a distance. WE KNEW ALL ALONG, they'd have said and shot at him from afar, twice, three, four, five times, dead.

Once the coast was clear, my father ran down from his hiding place. The plastic shoes already stank and with every step he took towards the tree and his father, he felt woozy from the stench of the shoes. That's how my father told it, but I don't think he felt woozy from the stench of the shoes, I think he felt woozy because of his father, who was dead and tied to the tree.

He said, My father's head hung forwards.

The soldiers had fired three shots into my grandfather's forehead. One shot in the head is enough to kill someone, but the soldiers in our region aren't sparing with their ammunition. Even though the commanding officer tells them, There's no point shooting all over the place. Sometimes the soldiers who shoot all over the place get beatings. Because the ones who shoot all over the place often miss their targets. And if you miss your target, you could end up in a trap and be shot dead yourself, the commanding officer tells his men. But in our region, soldiers fire twice. Sometimes even three, four, five times, to be doubly sure – three, four, five times over – that the target's really dead.

Before it was over, my grandfather said, I'M ALONE. Behind the rock, my father started to cry because he thought his father really meant it. I always really pitied him for that. I'm here, my father said. He was twenty-one years old. The soldiers said, Yes, we can see that. My father didn't move.

If we don't shoot, they'll shoot first. That's what the commanding officer said and that's what the soldier told his comrades up in the mountains. The comrades said, Terrorists who shoot must be shot dead. The commanding officer said, You have to protect your comrades. Imagine if my father had run down to his father. What would the soldiers have done? I'll tell you. They would have tied my father to the same tree – you can do damage with ropes – and shot him dead in front of his father. My father untied my grandfather from the tree. My grandfather was buried in the evening.

As long as I've been in the world, there have been soldiers. They didn't come into the world with me, of course; they were here before. But for as long as I can remember, I haven't been able to imagine life without them. These circumstances are a reaction to what has happened so far. They occupy a vast space in my life. The space is as vast as the country itself. What does that do to me? This is where logic gives out. You can't deny it. But the space remains the same. Just as big, I mean. The space remains just as big. So, it remains occupied. With soldiers who bring conflict with them and leave it here. It's not something you can just set aside. It does something to you.

My aunt, my father's sister, didn't witness this catastrophe. My aunt, her name was Gülten, got false papers and fled to Germany. In Germany, she didn't tell anyone where she'd come from. She had fled, which meant she could never come back. They had started looking for her here – not in Germany, but in this country.

On the telephone my aunt said, It's not the same.

First a warrant was issued, then she was sentenced to thirty-five years imprisonment in absentia. A secret witness, who would remain anonymous, was said to have testified against her. We never heard the witness statement. We read the charge on a slip of paper: *Separatism.* Then we read the number of years she was expected to spend behind bars. Then the secret witness went underground. In the end, my aunt had a heart attack. Not because of the persecution; it happened when she heard about her father's death. She lay on the floor of a flat in Germany for three days before she was found. Her body was returned to us in a coffin by aeroplane. My mother said, The end of every story is the home we return to. We threw flowers onto my aunt's body; the coffin was closed, earth fell onto it. Then we went back to the house. My father stood in the same spot for hours. His sister's grave lay next to his father's grave, he stood between them. Later, the funeral guests went back to their homes. It was getting dark but my father was still standing there. At some point, my mother dragged him inside. I told my brother, his name is Eren, I said, It doesn't matter. We won't say another word about this. Don't tell anyone about it, I said. But what did we know.

Who suffers the damage? Sometimes I think it's the others who suffer the damage, not the soldiers but those who have left. And of course, we suffer the damage too. But the damage grows with distance. You might find some peace and quiet in another country, but that's not to say you'll ever find real peace. After a disaster, that just isn't possible. I think the damage develops differently in a different country. In a different country far away from here, you understand more clearly what the damage has done. You can get to grips with total destruction. You dream of tanks and fire, policemen, officers, soldiers. Then you go to work. In fact, you only call to make sure there's no bad news. To make sure nothing's happened. You hang up and keep ringing round until everyone you know has had their turn. Then you start again from the beginning. When there were house searches, you sent the money that you'd earned in this country back to the country you'd had to leave. It never ends because the experience is constantly repeating itself.

My aunt always said, That's how we got here and that's how we'll go.
I said, We can't talk about it over the phone, Aunty.

She said, Devrim, sing something to distract me.

I always hated it when she said that on the phone. I often wouldn't do as she asked. When she died alone in Germany, I was sure she must have died with the receiver in her hand. You can never return to this country from another one. If you escape, you can't hide that you've done it, which means people here know. And then they want to know what you were running from. And when someone tells them what made you run away, they find themselves at the police station, then in prison. And we know that in this country you don't leave prison without being tortured. If you die in another country, you come back dead. Then they can't do any more damage. But the government can do damage. They do damage when they say, There is a terrorist in this coffin. A terrorist is coming back into our country. And then there are policemen, officers, soldiers outside the door again. Then they say, We dig up buried terrorists and then we burn them. No one wants to bury their dead far away. That's why our dead come home in coffins by aeroplane. It's like an interrogation coming to an end. It's only the end of the story that's clear. I'm quite sure my aunt had the receiver in her hand when she died.

My brother and I, we walked through fields and meadows every day. You could watch the army barracks from a spot high up. It was a big site. It was where they ate and slept and cleaned their guns. The soldiers held their G3s in their hands and we watched them. I said to my brother, They stroke their guns like dogs. The handier they are with the guns, the quicker they find their mark. The inexperienced soldiers have to keep watch; they're awake twenty-four hours a day, and if they fall asleep from exhaustion, they're instantly in battle, with terrorists behind rocks, and if the soldiers don't shoot, terrorists ambush and shoot them.

The experienced soldiers drag them out of sleep, on the ground; then the inexperienced soldiers wake with a start and reach straight for their guns and hold the guns in front of their chests in a panic. The experienced soldiers laugh and say, Did you think it was a terrorist? The inexperienced soldiers promise not to fall asleep again. Better to take greater pains to stay vigilant. Even if they're so tired they can no longer stand. They do it so that they don't get another scare. So that instead of sleeping, they'll shoot.

That evening, as Eren and I lay in bed, I said to Eren, We have to get going soon. Then we slept. Then we got up. When they started besieging our city, I shrugged. Our mother yelled, COME BACK INSIDE.

Then Eren and I set off for a relative's house. At the coach station I bought two tickets for Eren and me. Eren wanted a Pepsi, so I bought him one and we shared it between us. The coach station was full and I was scared that someone was following us. We hadn't done anything, but with the stories we'd heard, there was a shiver running up and down my back the whole time. You know, it can break your whole life in two. Take my aunt in Germany, for instance: she couldn't talk about anything else. Every time she called, she'd talk about it.

Devrim, I know they're waiting outside my door for me to leave the house, she'd say.

I couldn't understand why they would be waiting for my aunt to leave the house. They could just barge their way into her flat.

Why don't they just kill you and be done with it? I asked her. Being followed like this is the worst kind of torture, Devrim, you know that.

I know this because they followed my father too. I didn't actually want to talk about this. I'll have to keep it short. We were standing at this bus station. The Pepsi can was empty. The coach still hadn't arrived. And it was only then that I had to admit to myself that there had been a man following us for some time. He was around my father's age, perhaps. He was wearing dark trousers and a dark shirt, and over his shirt he wore a dark jacket. I know that lots of spies dress like civilians and they spy on people while disguised as civilians. They're government agents and they'll make you disappear. Eventually, the bus turned up. There was a big scramble. I groped for Eren's hand and quickly pulled him up the few steps behind me.

The coach driver asked, Are you travelling alone?
We're visiting our uncle, he's sick, I replied.
Good lads, he said.

The coach was full but we found an empty seat in the aisle. Eren sat on my lap; he looked out of the window and I looked at the coach driver and watched the passengers boarding. Eren was silent. I watched women with and without children mixing with the men who were getting on the coach. Old and young, some of them looked dangerous, some didn't. Sure enough, the man who had been watching us outside got on too. I put my arms around Eren's waist and held him tight.

The coach journey usually took four or five hours. Sometimes even six or seven, depending on the conditions and how well the roads were built. Two hours in, I gave Eren some bread. He didn't want to eat at first, but then he did, and then he fell asleep on my lap.

I thought things might be better when we made it to my uncle's house. When we arrived, we got off the coach quickly. I held onto Eren's hand; I felt a bit sorry for him, he wasn't as fast as me, so I hurried him along behind me until we were outside. At the coach station we had to catch a bus. The man I thought had been following us caught the bus too. I pretended I hadn't seen him. Our uncle was already waiting for us at the other bus station. The relief that spread through me, I can't describe it. Eren still hadn't spoken but when he saw our uncle, he ran up to him and said, *Uncle.* My legs were shaking. I thought of my aunt who died in Germany, because she reminded me of my uncle even though they weren't related. It was probably because they were a similar age. That really got to me. When my uncle hugged me, I whispered, That man's following us.

My father lived like this for a whole year. But we didn't find that out until later. We didn't even notice that there were spies among us. How could we? Imagine: you have a good friend for years and then years later you find out that he only seemed like a friend because he was tasked with spying on you. It's awful. I suppose we were just stupid. Because we were so careless. My parents gave the spies food and drink. They came and went as they pleased. January, February, March – they were round our house almost every day. Sometimes they even gave Eren and me gifts. Back then, it didn't bother me when strange people came to our house. My parents had lots of friends and were known for their hospitality. But now I think that the government in this country isn't interested in anything other than this war. April, May, June – the war was sitting on our chairs, hungry and thirsty, spooning up the soup that we were all eating. Their war was no longer just outside the door; it was hiding inside the house with all of us. August, September, October – the spies noted down and recorded everything. When I think back over it as I tell it to you, rage spreads inside me. And it's hardly surprising. Just imagine it: your good friend, who you've been friends with for years, gives you a compliment or consoles you when you cry, but then you find out they were a spy. In November and in December, too.

And the spy writes: *X goes red when complimented. X is quick to cry at unkind remarks.*

My mother was the first to grow suspicious. She didn't speak to my father about it, instead she wrote her suspicions on a piece of paper. He read what she'd written and said:

No, not those two.
She whispered, I can see it in their eyes.
They'd never do something like that, my father replied.

But my mother would be proved right in the end. The two men, we called them Kemal and Cengiz because that's how they introduced themselves, weren't called Kemal and Cengiz after all. I never learned their real names. It wasn't my father who discovered they were spies, but one of his friends, who was released after years in prison. Kemal and Cengiz were part of the unit that had arrested him back then. The news hadn't reached them that my father's friend had been released. My mother burst out laughing as the news spread. She said, *Life is so terrible. So terrible. Where else could something like this happen?* It happened every day for us. Then we had to check our flats for wires.

Sometimes when Kemal brought me presents, he'd say hello to my parents and then come into my room. He'd stay there for some time. He would always stay a good while. The gifts were always lavishly wrapped. Pretty wrapping paper. Sometimes with polka dots. Sometimes in single colours. Green, for instance, or red or yellow. There were also lots with animal patterns. Horses, for instance, donkeys and dogs. I was a child and I was glad of any present. We didn't get many presents back then. We went to school, came home and often couldn't leave the flat because of the fighting. We were poor and any toy made me happy. I'd like to take it all back now. If I'd known everything I know now, I would have leapt off Kemal's lap and battered him with his own presents.

Kemal sat next to me on the floor. He often pulled me onto his lap, I didn't like it but he wouldn't let me go, he'd say, Stay with your Uncle Kemal. Then he'd watch me unwrap the present. My parents would say, Give your Uncle Kemal a hug, and I would hug him. I'd climb off his lap and Kemal would stay there sitting beside me. Even after I'd unwrapped the present. And even after the hug. I can't really remember what it was like or when it started. But at some point he started to ask me questions about my father. Your dad doesn't come straight home from work on some days, does he? At the time, my father was working in a plastic bag factory. I shrugged. He had two shifts at the factory. One early in the morning and one in the early evening. At midday, he came home to sleep. We hadn't seen him that often since he'd had that job. If he was asleep, we'd come home and wouldn't wake him. In the evenings, he'd put us to bed and then he'd go back to work. You know, I'm very attached to my parents. To my mother and to my father.

Do you know where he goes?
Why are you asking? I asked Kemal once.
He said, I really like your dad.

Before Kemal and Cengiz disappeared back onto the bus they'd arrived on, Kemal yelled in the middle of the street:

THE DOGS HAVE ATTACKED.
WE KNOW WHO YOU ARE.

My father covered my ears. One part of me stayed with my mother and one part stayed with my father. Now I have nothing left, of them or of me. I knew what was in store for us. We had to leave town because of Kemal and Cengiz. If there were spies among us then sooner or later there would be soldiers too.

We always said, First come the spies, then the soldiers.
They say, Every man in this country is born a soldier.

This all happened on the same day. Special units moved in and stormed our region. I was told that Kemal and Cengiz were running through the streets, pointing at houses and saying, THERE, IN THERE – the special unit followed them at every turn and Kemal and Cengiz continued along as the special units behind them charged into the houses. THERE AND

THERE – and so it went on. In the end, the entire block was cleared and seventy-five people were arrested.

Eren and I were already on the way to the coach station by then. Our aunt fled to Germany and we went to our uncle's. It took me a long time to get used to the situation.

Our uncle made up his bedroom for us. There was a bed and a mattress on the floor. Since Eren was the younger of the two of us, he got to sleep in the bed and I took the mattress on the floor. My uncle had been sleeping on the sofa in the living room since we'd arrived. We would go to bed early in the evening and I'd get up very early in the morning. Then I'd usually walk around in circles while Eren slept. There was no other way of enduring the powerlessness. I didn't see my uncle's wife, her name was Fidan, once during our stay. Every day it was on the tip of my tongue, but I didn't ask my uncle about her. For fear it would break his heart. My uncle told the neighbour that he was ill and we'd come to look after him. What good young lads you are, the neighbour said when she saw me in the lift with a bag of shopping. My uncle is very ill, I replied. Poor little boy, she said, and I got out of the lift.

My uncle didn't talk much. He cooked our food, washed our clothes, tucked us in at night. When Eren was asleep, I would get up again and go to him in the living room. My uncle would cry, and I'd cry with him. I could no longer tell how long it had been since I had seen my parents. A few years had passed by then.

Please can I call my parents, I'd ask over and over.
I'm sorry, Devrim. The lines are tapped.

The man from the bus station didn't let up, not even now we were far away. To this day I still don't know if it was because of my mother or because of my father. My father disappeared before we set off to stay with our uncle. If a spy is on your back, you can be sure that something's going to happen to you sooner or later. And my father thought that if he left us, we would be spared. If only it were that easy. One evening he came into our room while I was sleeping and woke me up. He didn't turn the light on but his silhouette was clear enough to make out. He pulled me to him and hugged me for a very long time. The chain he wore around his neck – it was a thin silver chain with a small locket, and inside the locket was a picture of me and Eren – he put it around my neck and kissed my forehead. Then my cheeks. They were wet with his tears. I thought it was stupid to give me a chain with a picture of me and Eren hanging on it because I already knew what Eren and I looked like. That was all I could think in that moment. Eren was asleep and I was awake. It happened before I could even grasp what was going on: my father was leaving us. I wrapped my arms around his middle. I didn't need a picture of Eren and me, I needed one of him.

My father said, Don't forget who we are.

My father had to leave town. My aunt fled to Germany to be safe, and we went to stay with our uncle, who did nothing but cry all the time. Eren was asleep when my father stroked his head, before he left our flat that night, when it was so dark that I couldn't see anything. As he pulled the flat door shut behind him – the way he always did when he left for the factory, so as not to wake us up – I whispered, My father has gone out. The spy would write: *A terrorist is on the move.* That was the last time I saw my father. But who was I speaking to? Maybe to Eren, he was asleep. On the chain around my neck hangs a picture of me and my brother, and now I'm with my brother at my uncle's house.

The man who came into our lives at the bus station never disappeared from our lives. At first I thought it was me he was after, but then at some point he started following my uncle. My uncle would leave the house in the morning drenched in sweat, and drenched in sweat was how he would return each evening.

The spy would write: *X starts work at 06:15. X leaves the factory at 19:00.*

My uncle knew the stories. You go to work in the morning, then the professionals turn up: a shot to the head, dead, and you're left lying in the street. Sometimes you're not found until the evening because everyone was working and no one realised you were missing. My uncle was more afraid of being struck down in the middle of the street with a shot to the head than disappearing altogether.

When he disappeared from my life, for me a life disappeared with him. My uncle walked home from work, like he did every day, drenched in sweat. The car was already following him when he left the factory for the flat. If he walked faster, then the car sped up; if he walked slower, then the car slowed down. My uncle came through the door with his eyes wide. Eren and I were sitting on the sofa in the kitchen; he knelt on the floor in front of us, grabbed Eren by the shoulders and said, We are your family, don't forget that. Then he stood up, walked to the kitchen cupboard, took out a sheet of paper and a pen and wrote something on it with trembling hands. Then he turned to me and held out the piece of paper. He said, Devrim, Devrim, his voice shook like his hands did. Memorise what it says here. He was so distraught that I started to sweat. I couldn't take my eyes off my uncle's face, it was so distorted with fear that it frightened me. On the paper was an address. Memorise it, memorise it, he howled. I read it line by line. The street. Devrim, you mustn't forget this, Devrim. The house number. Devrim, concentrate.

I said, I've memorised it.

Then my uncle ran to the kitchen sink in a panic, put the paper in the sink and set fire to it with a lighter. He said, You've got two minutes to pack your things. I grabbed my brother's hand. Devrim, please, said my uncle, please, they're coming. In the bedroom, I took my rucksack out of the cupboard, shoved trousers, socks, underpants and two knitted jumpers inside. When I was done, I ran back into the kitchen. Eren was still sitting on the sofa. The crisis was climbing out of uniforms and into the flat. Straight into me and my brother. That night, I took the chain my father had given me before he struck out in the middle of the night, and I fastened it around my little brother's neck. I wasn't sure what was going to happen, I said, Why can't you come? My uncle grabbed my wrist and pulled me to him. They're looking for you, he whispered. The tears that Eren was crying, I understood them now.

I said, This is supposed to be over.

I climbed over the balcony, two floors down the flat's façade.

My uncle whispered after me in the dark, like my father had, Don't forget who we are. I'd never forget. Not my uncle, not my brother, or my father or my mother or my aunt who cried on the telephone because she was in Germany and not with us.

I ran to the bus station and bought a ticket; at some point, the bus came and I got on. This time, I sat by the window. I didn't talk to anyone and I didn't look at anyone. For most of the journey I pretended to be asleep, but I wasn't. From the window, I watched the streets as they carried me away again. I thought of my father and my aunt. I don't know where my parents are. My brother is with my uncle. I'm on a bus. The journey takes over seven hours. It's the afternoon by the time I get in.

We don't tell anyone who we are. You'd think that means we're safe, but we're not. We don't tell anyone who we are. But we don't forget who we are. And then we end up here. And that's how a never-ending story ends in one lifetime. And a different story is told twice, in two parts: in the West and in the East. But now I'm in this tower block. Far from the past.

Eleven years have gone by and suddenly I see my mother again. This is our life too. And I see the man who drags her out the door. Ayten is on the ground. What does it matter how much time has passed? BERO, I want to scream, Bero, my good little boy, how far apart we were; he's lying in a pool of blood. But I don't move, I just look at my mother. She's in hand-cuffs. There's a watchman next to her. When she sees me, she recognises me at once and says, MY GOD, ALL DOGS DIE. Please don't get me wrong. The spy would write: *All dogs really do have to die.* In my rucksack, on top of the knitted jumpers my mother gave me eleven years ago, there is a gun. I take the gun out of my rucksack. The spy would write: *X has seen her son. X is crying.* I take a step towards my mother. The spy would write: *Children of terrorists become terrorists too.* That's how they explain how things turn out in this country. But they've stopped thinking about the violence they carry within them. And the bombs they plant fly out of the air and into our homes. An unexploded bomb can be disarmed. But even a disarmed bomb was a bomb once. The watchman is standing next to my mother, next to my mother on the ground sits Ayten, and next to Ayten on the ground lies Bero, in a pool of blood. I pull the trigger.